PRAISE FOR DIANA PALMER

"Nobody tops Diana Palmer
when it comes to delivering pure,
undiluted romance. I love her stories."
—*New York Times* bestselling author Jayne Ann Krentz

"Diana Palmer is a mesmerizing storyteller who
captures the essence of what a romance should be."
—*Affaire de Coeur*

"Diana Palmer is a unique talent
in the romance industry. Her writing
combines wit, humor, and sensuality;
and, as the song says, nobody does it better!"
—*New York Times* bestselling author Linda Howard

"No one beats this author for sensual anticipation."
—*Rave Reviews*

"A love story that is pure and enjoyable."
—*Romantic Times* on *Lord of the Desert*

"The dialogue is charming, the characters
likeable and the sex sizzling..."
—*Publishers Weekly* on *Once in Paris*

Diana Palmer has published over seventy category romances, as well as historical romances and longer contemporary works. With over forty million copies of her books in print, *New York Times* bestselling author Diana Palmer is one of North America's most beloved authors. Her accolades include seven national Waldenbooks bestseller awards, four national B. Dalton bestseller awards, two Bookrak national sales awards, a Lifetime Achievement Award for series storytelling from *Romantic Times* magazine, several *Affaire de Coeur* awards and two regional RWA awards. Diana resides in the north mountains of her home state of Georgia with her husband, James, and their son, Blayne Edward.

DIANA PALMER

Dream's End

Published by Silhouette Books
America's Publisher of Contemporary Romance

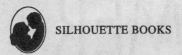 SILHOUETTE BOOKS

ISBN 0-373-51280-5

DREAM'S END

First published as a MacFadden Romance
by Kim Publishing Corporation.

Copyright © 1979 by Diana Palmer.

Visit Silhouette at www.eHarlequin.com

Printed in U.S.A.

One

Eleanor Perrie peeked up from her typing. The distinguished man in the gray business suit had begun shifting restlessly on the luxurious couch. He seemed to be checking his watch every minute. She permitted herself a tiny smile before she touched the intercom button between the living room, where she worked, and the stables down below the big ranch house.

"What is it?" came the impatient reply.

"I think your souffle is done," she said, purposefully vague. "It's very puffed and browning off on top."

There was soft, deep laughter just for an instant on the other end of the line. She could almost see the grin on that swarthy face. "I'll be right up, Miss Perrie."

"I sincerely hope so, Mr. Matherson," she replied with sugary sarcasm, and cut off the connection. She glanced at the man in the gray suit and smiled. Her creamy complexion lit up and emphasized the odd pale green of her eyes, hidden by over-sized round eyeglasses with black frames. Her jet black hair was coiled and pinned on top of her head.

"Mr. Matherson will be right up," she said courteously, raising her voice now so that he could hear her from across the room.

"Thank you," the impatient man said stiffly.

"One of our prize Appaloosa mares

was foaling this morning,'' Eleanor added for effect. ''Mr. Matherson wanted to see about her.''

''I understand,'' the older man nodded, with a polite smile that didn't reach his eyes.

Oh, no, you don't, Eleanor thought with amusement as she dropped her eyes back to the letter she was typing. Curry Matherson knew how to get what he wanted from people, and this poor little fish was about to find it out. Curry had planned to build a very sophisticated office complex on land that belonged to this annoyed speculator. The whole deal hinged on whether or not Durwood Magins, sitting nervously on the very edge of the big sofa, could be persuaded to sell at a fair market price—not the exorbitant figure he was demanding.

Tired of bargaining with him, this morning Curry had called Magins to tell him he was dropping the whole project and had found another site. Fifteen minutes later, Magins had been sitting on the same sofa he was glued to now. And Curry, who was only looking at the new foal, not helping to deliver it, had allowed him to sit there and sweat it out for two solid hours. Eleanor watched the greedy little man with mingled compassion and amusement. His own avarice seemed to her to be his worst enemy. And he should have had the sense not to tangle with Curry in the first place. This was really one of her boss's nicer tactics.

Seconds later, Curry Matherson walked into the room. There was a half smile on his lean, tanned face that was at variance with the glittering, quite dangerous look in his silvery eyes. He towered over most people, and since Magins wasn't tall anyway, Curry made him look like a dwarf. Her boss's athletic body was built with hard riding and ranch work, as well as sports, at which he excelled. Curry excelled at everything.

She tried not to look at him too hard

as he shook Magins' hand with a grip that probably bruised it, but her eyes kept going back to him, tracing the hard lines of his face, the thick dark hair that was just a little unruly from the wind. She'd loved him forever, it seemed. Since the day she applied for the job as his private secretary three years ago....

He hadn't been in a good mood at all on the morning of her interview, and Eleanor had been a little bit afraid of the tall, dark man. If she hadn't just lost her parents, and suddenly discovered how badly off she was going to be financially, and needed a job in such a desperate hurry, she'd probably have walked out the door.

Looking back, she couldn't help but smile at her own determination. She was fourth in line to be interviewed. The three women who preceded her had been experienced and neatly dressed—one of them was a raving beauty. All were older than her very nervous eighteen years.

And there were four more waiting to be interviewed, equally equipped with brains and beauty.

Eleanor had been wearing a simple mint green cotton shirtwaist dress with white sandals. Her hair was coiled on top of her head because she thought the severe style made her look older, and her eyes were surrounded by a pair of unstylish black eyeglasses that made her look owlish. She only needed the glasses for close work, but they were a kind of security blanket and she wore them all the time, like camouflage. She'd never tried to emphasize her looks—she didn't believe she had any, thanks to the effort of her devoutly religious mother to keep her "unpainted." She'd never dated a man, or been kissed by one, and her evenings at home had been filled with chores numerous enough to make dating impossible even if she'd been interested in it.

Curry had barely spared her a glance when she walked into his office and sat down in the chair across from his massive, polished oak desk. He sat there with his eyes on what presumably was her résumé, and she wondered at his powerful physique, at the black hair threaded with gray, the dark complexion, and was knocked for a loop when he looked up directly into her eyes and she saw that his were silver. Not gray, not blue—silver, polished and glittery. She didn't even hear his first question, she was so fascinated by him.

"I said," he repeated with a calm that did nothing to disguise his impatience, "what kind of experience do you have? It isn't listed here," he added, waving the sheet of paper at her.

She straightened her thin shoulders. "I was my father's secretary at home after I finished school," she recalled, the memory making her sad. "I kept his books and handled all his correspondence."

He leaned back in his swivel chair, lighting a cigarette as he studied her through narrowed eyes—disapproving eyes, she thought suddenly.

"You're not even out of your teens, are you, Miss…" he looked at the résumé and back up at her "…Perrie?"

She lifted her chin proudly. "I'm eighteen, Mr. Matherson."

"Eighteen," he murmured, his eyes sweeping what was visible of her about the level of the desk. "Got a boyfriend, Miss Perrie?"

She shook her head.

"Why not?" he asked nonchalantly, leaning forward on his elbows to pin her with those strange eyes. "Don't you like sex?"

She drew in a shocked breath, and her pale eyes widened.

His face relaxed suddenly, and his silvery eyes danced as he smiled at her. "I won't have to chase you out of my bed, will I, Eleanor Perrie?" he asked. "Or dodge from having you throw yourself at me?"

"That sounds like conceit to me, Mr. Matherson," she replied with a cool, steady tone despite her screaming emotions. "You're not *that* attractive, with all due respect, and you're years too old, anyway."

His eyebrows went up. "My God, little girl, how old do you think I am?" he exclaimed.

She studied him for a long moment, her eyes touching, for some inexplicable reason, the fine, chiseled line of his mouth. "Oh, at least thirty," she replied with irrepressible honesty.

His brows collided and he scowled. "I'm thirty-two, as it happens. But until now, I didn't know that put me on the waiting list for the local old age home."

She smiled shyly and dropped her eyes.

He laughed again, softly. "Spring flower," he murmured. "Little jade bud. How can I turn you down?"

She looked up. "I'm hired?" she asked incredulously.

"We all have moments of unexplained weakness," he replied. "You do realize that a private secretary lives in? I have a passion for dictation at one o'clock in the morning while I watch the Johnny Carson show."

"That's all right," she replied. "I like staying up late."

"Most children do," he told her with an amused smile, and laughed outright at the look that chilled her face.

It had been the beginning of a long, rewarding partnership. Eleanor knew him as few other women ever got to. She saw him tired, angry, happy, playful, bored, even rarely discouraged. She saw him as only a wife would ordinarily, in all kinds of conditions, at all times of the night and day. And gradually, so gradually that she wasn't even aware of it, she grew to love him. Despite his women, and he had them, plenty of them, she never looked at another man. With her hair still in its coil, her glasses still in place, with new frames identical to the old ones every year, the same simple country girl kind of dresses, she was no threat to any of his heart-throbs. They didn't see Eleanor as any kind of competition, and they confided in her, hoping it would get them close to Curry. But, of course, it didn't. At the end of the affair, Curry would have her send a dozen yellow roses from the florist. It was an unspoken thing, a quiet rejection, that was as final as death. And a few weeks later, he'd be off in pursuit of someone else.

He liked sophisticated women. Beautiful, sleek, well-groomed women who knew it all. She'd never seen him date anything less. Oh, Eleanor went with him to an occasional party in the line of duty—but it was always in something simple, she never wore makeup or changed her hair or took off her glasses. Whether or not that was intentional, she didn't stop to ask herself. The relationship she had with her boss, while platonic, was satisfying and delightful. She didn't want to rock the boat by admitting how deeply her feelings went. She'd learned long ago never to want very much. Disappointment had taught her the dangers of caring too deeply.

Her mind came back to the present just as Curry finished talking with Magins, shook his hand, thanked him for his co-operation and shoveled him out the door.

"You are," she told Curry, "a pirate. You'd have been right at home on the Spanish Main, hanging people from yard-arms."

He raised an amused eyebrow at her. "Probably," he admitted, lifting his lighted cigarette to his lips. "What's wrong, Jadebud, your conscience bother-ing you?"

"Thanks to you, I don't have one," she shot back at him. "I've been corrupted."

He laughed outright. "No doubt. How about calling Mandy for me? Tell her I'll be a little late picking her up tonight. Jack Smith's ready to talk terms on that prize filly I've been after for two months.''

''How's Amanda going to take that?'' Eleanor asked dryly. ''I mean when I tell her she's been stood up for a horse?''

His eyes narrowed sensuously. ''I'll soothe her ruffled feelings later,'' he said in a soft tone.

Eleanor felt ripples of jealousy wash over her, but she was too practiced to let any emotion show. She smiled instead. ''I'll call her. What time do I tell her to expect you?''

He turned and started for the door. ''Make it seven,'' he called over his shoulder.

She glared after him, at that dark, masculine arrogance he wore like a cloak around his muscular body. He'd been going with Amanda Mitchell for well over six months, a new record for one of his relationships, but if he felt much of anything for the gorgeous titian-haired model, it didn't affect him in any obvious way. He could leave her hanging like this, and had, many times, without a single qualm. He took her for granted, just as he took Eleanor and everybody else around him for granted. Arrogance, and Eleanor wondered how Amanda put up with it. The model could have had any of a dozen men by snapping her fingers, but the only one she wanted was Curry. And by being cunning—and probably by holding out— she'd landed him. Temporarily, at least. Eleanor didn't take the affair seriously. It was just one more conquest for Curry, that was all.

She dialed Amanda and gave her the news.

"Just like a man," came the musical reply, and Eleanor could almost see the amused look on Amanda's thin face. "Honestly, if Curry could forget horses for just five minutes..." She sighed. "Eleanor, how do you stand it?" she asked sympathetically.

"I have a nervous breakdown once a week, religiously." Eleanor laughed. She couldn't help liking the red-headed model; everybody did, she was so vivacious and open-hearted.

"I believe it. All right, tell the incorrigible brute I'll wait. Not," she added, "that he deserves it."

"I'll tell him that, too." Eleanor laughed.

"I dare you," Amanda teased. "Don't you know Curry would faint if you ever talked back to him? Why do you let him walk on you the way he does? It's outrageous what you take!"

"It goes with the job, I've been doing it a long time. Besides, what would his ranch hands say if he fainted?" Eleanor replied.

Amanda sighed. "I give up. See you."

"Bye."

Eleanor sighed, shaking her head. It was true; Curry could be hard to get along with. But sometimes, he could be charm personified. Especially when he wanted her to work overtime.

Curry had already gone to see the filly when a late model Buick drove up the front steps.

Jim Black was a head shorter than Curry, just about Eleanor's own height, burly and just a little overweight, with a leonine face and dark eyes. He was smiling, and his eyes twinkled as they met Eleanor's.

"I thought you might feel like having supper," he said.

She laughed. "As a matter of fact, Bessie had a church meeting tonight, and I'd be eating alone," she replied.

"When I get through stealing you," Jim told her gaily, "Bessie Mills is next on my list. Of all the cooks in the county, Curry has the best one."

"Curry always has the best, didn't you know that?" Eleanor laughed.

"You're the best, too, Norie." Jim grinned. "Why won't you come work for me? I pay better than Curry, and I'd even give you two days a week off. That's two more than you get from Curry.''

"Don't tempt me," she said with a smile. "Are we going out, or do you want me to cook you something here?"

"Out, woman, of course," he exclaimed. "You work hard enough as it is."

"I don't really," she protested.

"Will you go and get dressed?" he sighed.

She held out her arms, gesturing toward the pale yellow dress. "Why can't I go like this?"

"Because I'm taking you to the Limelight Club," he replied patiently. "And I'd love, just once, to see you dressed to the hilt."

She stared at him. "Me?"

His dark eyes narrowed. "You. Why not try a night out without your camouflage? Curry won't see you, I guarantee it."

"You're asking a lot," she murmured. "Why?"

"Just curiosity. Aren't we friends enough for me to be a little curious, Norie?" he asked gently.

"Well..."

"Be daring! Think of yourself as Mata Hari, feverishly pursuing state secrets!"

She laughed in spite of herself. "Well, maybe...I do have a gown I've never worn."

"You could let your hair down, too, and take off those horrible glasses you don't need."

She gaped at him. "What are you up to?" she asked suspiciously.

He looked vaguely uncomfortable. As long as she'd known Jim, he'd never been able to keep a secret from her. They were only friends, but it was a close kind of friendship, and she genuinely cared about him.

"Jim, what is it?" she probed softly, her green eyes holding his intently.

He smirked. "All right, I need a little help. Just a little, just this once," he said quickly.

Her eyes widened and she smiled. "Why you old rooster," she laughed. "You want to make someone jealous!"

He turned beet red. "Well..."

She laughed. "Jim, my friend, for you I'll do the very best I can. But don't expect miracles," she called over her shoulder. "For that you need good raw material to start with!"

She had gowns and she kept makeup, but tonight was the first time in her life she'd ever tried deliberately to look attractive. It was new, and a little frightening, and she had a sudden premonition that things would change beyond recognition if she went through with it. But after all, Jim had never turned his back on her when she needed help. He was every bit as rich as Curry, but so much more approachable. And she owed it to him. She began to take down her hair.

Two

___

She took out the long, white chiffon gown she'd been saving for a rainy day. It was low cut in a V-neck, sleeveless and fell seductively around her slender figure. Her feet were encased in white high-heeled sandals with a beading of rhinestones on the straps.

She sat down in front of her mirror, looking curiously at the stranger she saw there—her long, waving hair tumbling down around her shoulders, her eyes bigger and more feminine without the protective glasses. She applied just a touch of eye shadow and lipstick. And when she was through, she stared at herself with astonishment. Remembering her mother's valiant efforts to keep her from using ''paint'' or emphasizing her assets, she felt a pang of pure guilt at the way she looked. There was a sensuous air about her that had never been apparent before, and the white chiffon left a lot of soft, honey-colored skin bare. Before she could change her mind about it, she grabbed her lacy shawl and pearl clutch bag and hurried downstairs.

Jim turned when he heard her footsteps and froze where he stood at the bottom of the staircase, looking up at her as if he'd never seen a woman before.

''Well,'' he said finally, on a hard sigh. ''Well, well! I don't think I've ever seen anything that could top that transformation,'' he said, shaking his head. ''Norie, have you always looked like that, or do you have some magical device upstairs?''

"A fairy godmother," she whispered conspiratorially. "But don't tell anyone."

"Cinderella, is it?" He laughed. "Come hop into my horseless carriage, you gorgeous thing, and I'll take you to the ball!"

She did feel like Cinderella, even if Jim's sleek blue convertible wasn't exactly a golden coach. He took her to the Limelight Club, one of the better restaurants. They sat in a private alcove surrounded by live plants.

Looking at her, Jim shook his head and sighed, his dark eyes still disbelieving. "I knew you were pretty," he said with his usual candor, "but I didn't know you were a potential Miss World. Why the rags and cinders all this time, Cinderella?" he asked.

She shrugged. "I've never wanted to impress anyone," she admitted with a tiny smile. "My mother was devoutly religious. She felt that vanity was the greatest sin, and she taught me to under-emphasize my assets."

"Does it embarrass you to look pretty?" he asked.

She blushed. "I didn't know I did."

He laughed. "I'm glad I had this idea," he remarked, letting his eyes trace her lovely features, her smooth shoulders.

"Who are we working on?" she asked as the waiter left their menus and went away.

"Her," he said quickly, nodding toward a woman who'd just come in on the arm of a much older man.

Without being obvious, Eleanor half turned in her seat and got a glimpse of a lovely young blonde, as delicate looking as a rosebud, with a knockout figure.

"Who is she?" she whispered.

"The daughter of the man who owns the club—that's her father with her." He grinned suddenly and turned his attention back to the menu. "I think we've been spotted. Don't look, but she's really giving you a green-eyed look."

"Aha, that's why you brought me here, to be stabbed in the back." She smiled.

"In a sense. You're a real pal, Norie. I'll do you a good turn one of these days," he promised faithfully.

"No need. I love playing cupid. Is she still glaring?"

"Sure is...oh, my gosh!" His face drew up.

"What's wrong?"

"Hide behind your menu for a minute, quick!" Jim said.

"Why?" she whispered.

"Because Curry and Amanda just walked through the door!"

She felt herself sinking down in the leather booth. Frightened suddenly, for no good reason, she quickly pulled the menu up to conceal her face, leaving her shoulders and a glimpse of her long hair visible.

"Hello, Jim!" came Curry's deep voice. "Haven't seen you in a long time."

"You're never home when I call at the ranch." Jim laughed. "I get over a good bit to see Norie."

"Norie," Curry scoffed. "My God, what a name. She looks like an Eleanor; pet names don't suit her."

"You call her Jadebud," Jim countered.

"In my good moods, when I want something," Curry said darkly. "Eleanor's not much to look at, even though she's a damned good secretary. I flatter her a little now and then. It doesn't hurt and," he added with a heartless smile, "it helps keep her efficiency up."

"Curry, how can you talk like that about her?" Amanda scolded gently and Eleanor, listening helplessly, hurting, blessed her for it. "After all, she's been with you for three years!"

"She'll be with me forever," Curry

said nonchalantly. "Where else does she have to go? No man will ever want her, that's for damned sure, and I pay good wages. What else does the little spinster need?"

"Someone better than you to work for," Jim said with sudden, hot anger, and Eleanor knew without looking that those dark eyes would be narrow with it. "She's never had a vacation, did you notice? She never takes time off at all, she just bows down to you as you pass by her. Someday she won't be there for you to walk all over, Curry, and what will you do then?"

Curry's voice deepened as it always did in anger. "Are you still trying to steal her, Black?"

"Any way I can, Curry," he replied gruffly. "I may not be as colorful to work for as you are, but I'll treat her decently and that's something you've never done!"

There was a short, tense pause. "How

would you like to step around back with me?'' Curry asked huskily.

"Any time," Jim replied tightly.

"Now, boys," Amanda said gently, "this isn't the time or the place. Let's just enjoy the meal, okay?"

Eleanor felt the tension slowly relax, and she knew her fingers were trembling where they held the menu.

"Let it pass," Curry said roughly. "But, Black, you stay the hell away from my spread."

"With pleasure," Jim ground out. "Watch your nose, while you're about it, Curry. If it rains, you'll drown."

Jim waited until Curry and Amanda were a few steps away before he took down the menu Eleanor was using as a shield. His face grew tighter when he saw the tears misting her soft green eyes.

"Let's get the hell out of here," he told her. "I've lost my appetite."

She only nodded, throwing her wrap around her shoulders as she stood up. She felt a strange tingling at the back of her neck as she and Jim started out of the Club. It wasn't until they were outside that she dared dart a glance backwards to see Curry staring after them. She kept her face carefully averted and followed Jim to the parking lot.

"The damned high-handed son of a..." Jim was muttering as they pulled up in front of the ranch house after a light supper at a restaurant smaller than the club.

"Don't strain yourself," Eleanor said with forced lightness. "Curry isn't worth it, he really isn't."

"Now will you come work for me?" Jim asked flatly.

She nodded. "Just give me a day or two to work out the details and give Curry his two weeks' notice."

"All right. Norie, I'm so sorry you had to hear that," he said gently, brushing the hair away from her flushed cheeks.

"I'm not. I only wish I'd known three

years ago," she said miserably. "Good night, Jim."

"Good night, Cinderella. I hope the ball wasn't too bad."

She kissed him on the cheek. "The handsome prince wasn't bad at all," she teased as she got out of the car. "I hope your young lady gets jealous enough to call you up and propose."

"She might at that, you lovely creature. Good night!"

She watched him drive away with a feeling of loss, of sweeping aloneness. With a sigh, her dreams shattered, her hopes in ruins, she turned and went into the house and up to her room. And she cried herself to sleep.

In the morning, she put the camouflage back on and went down to breakfast. Curry had already had his coffee and toast and headed out to wait for Smith to deliver the new filly, Bessie told her.

The buxom housekeeper sat down at

the table with Eleanor and sipped her own coffee.

"Came in late last night, he did, must have been four in the morning," Bessie remarked. "I barely heard him and looked at the clock. Out with that redhead again, I'll bet."

"With Amanda? Yes, I think so," Eleanor said vaguely.

"She's no country girl," Bessie sighed, cupping her reddened hands around the mug of coffee. "If he marries her, he'll be sorry. Won't want kids, either, if I don't miss my guess. Too proud of that slim figure."

"You have to admit, she's the nicest one so far," Eleanor said tightly, wishing Bessie could talk about something else.

"That isn't saying much."

"She loves him."

"Like fun," Bessie scoffed. "She loves his money, and maybe she likes the way he is in..." She stopped, flushing.

"Bed?" Eleanor finished for her.

Bessie shrugged her heavy shoulders. "None of my business."

"None of mine, either," the younger girl said with a smile.

She went into the living room and sat down behind the desk. She was sorting the correspondence that needed answering when Curry came into the room.

"Good morning, Jadebud," he said brightly, looking younger than he had in weeks.

She spared him a glance, feeling the wound open up at the sight of him, and wondered how she was going to break the news to him. Her heart began to race nervously.

"Good morning," she replied nonchalantly.

His eyes narrowed. "Is something wrong, Eleanor?"

He rarely called her by name. It made her tingle when he said her name like that, but she stiffened and held onto her resolution. "I...I wanted to ask you..."

"I've got something to tell you, too."
He drew out a cigarette and lit it. "Now's
as good a time as any. I asked Amanda
to marry me last night. She said yes."

Three

It was like dying, Eleanor thought suddenly. Just exactly how it must feel to die. The quick, sharp blow vibrating through her body and all of life and love and color draining out in an invisible pool on the floor beside her chair. The cruel words she'd heard last night were nothing compared to this. Nothing!

She knew her face would be pale, but she kept her eyes from showing anything, hoping he was far enough away that he wouldn't see the sudden wounding in her quick pulse and unsteady breathing.

His eyes narrowed. "Didn't you hear what I just told you?" he asked curtly. "I'm getting married."

Her eyebrows went up. "I heard you," she said carelessly, and forced a smile onto her lips. "Give me time, I'm trying to think up some condolences to send to Amanda."

He made a half smile at that, but something was troubling him. It showed in the turbulence of his silver eyes as he studied her through wisps of gray, curling smoke.

"Eleanor," he said quietly, "you won't leave me?"

She licked her pink lips nervously and dropped her eyes to her typewriter. "I...I've been trying to find some way to tell you," she faltered, "that I've had... another offer."

"You've had other offers ever since I brought you here," he said roughly.

"From Batsen, Boster, even from Jim Black. Which one is it? Black?" he asked ominously.

"Yes," she replied calmly, lifting her face to catch the flare of anger in his dark eyes. "Please," she said softly, "I've been here three years. You can't really expect me to stay forever. There's a whole world out there, Mr. Matherson, and all I've ever seen of it is my parents' home and then yours. I've never been out on my own, I've never had the kind of freedom that you and other people take for granted. I've got to decide what to do with my life. I can't do it here!"

His eyes narrowed, and she saw his square jaw lock and she knew she was going to be in for a fight. "You've been doing it," he snapped. "What's the matter, honey, don't I pay you enough? Do you think you're worth more?"

He studied her insolently, his eyes whipping over her slender body in the shapeless dress as she rose to stand unsteadily beside the desk. "My God, you wouldn't bring five dollars on auction, you little chicken! What do you think you're going to find out there, some man blind enough to want you?"

Nothing, ever, had hurt her as much as those last cold words. It was just Curry, furious and meaning to hurt, to get even. But that didn't register, not on top of what she'd overheard last night. She felt as if he'd put a knife into her and twisted it. She couldn't stop the tears that welled hot and flooding in her eyes.

She turned and walked toward the door, not looking at him, not speaking.

"Where are you going, you scrawny ostrich?" he growled. "To hide your head in the sand?"

She opened the door and walked out into the hall, blind to the appearance of Bessie, who stood there as if she'd been struck dumb. There had never been a cross word between Eleanor and Curry, not in three years.

"What about those reservations for my Miami trip, Miss Perrie?" he said from the doorway of the living room, his voice harsh and unpleasant.

Eleanor had her hand on the banister and she turned, with tears running down her cheeks, her slender body shaking with mingled rage and humiliation.

"If you want the damned reservations, you call for them," she told him fiercely. "And you've got my two weeks' notice right now!"

She whirled, ignoring the shock on his face, and ran upstairs.

She stayed in her room for the rest of the day. All day, without moving from the chair by her window, from which she could watch the Appaloosas dancing in their paddocks, the prize black Angus cattle grazing on the meadows that stretched flat and green to the horizon.

She wanted to go downstairs and throw something heavy at the arrogant cattle rancher. Three years of putting up with

his temper and his tirades, of standing between him and the whole world, of
smoothing his path, making his stupid
reservations, sending flowers and cards
and gifts to his women, keeping up with
his correspondence, being dragged out of
bed at two in the morning to write a letter
about a bull he wanted to buy. All that,
for three years, and in five minutes he'd
forced her out of his life. Perhaps, she
thought miserably, he'd even done it on
purpose.

With his uncanny knack of reading her,
it was possible he'd guessed how she felt
and was making it easier for her to go.
She'd rather have thought that than to
have thought he'd cared so little about
her that he could insult her so easily.

Chicken. Ostrich. Wouldn't bring five
dollars at auction. Find a man blind
enough to want her. Her eyes closed on
the painful words. He'd never spoken to
her like that before. He'd ranted and
raved, and lost his gunpowder temper,

and growled at her slowness when he was pacing the room waiting for some typing. But he'd never made his remarks personal, he'd never touched her, or tried to. It had been a non-physical relationship from the very beginning. It had been a comradeship. Until today, when he finally decided to tell the truth and let her know what he really thought of her as a woman.

Fighting tears, she reached for the telephone and dialed Jim Black's number.

When he answered, a sob involuntarily tore out of her throat. "Jim?" she asked huskily.

"Norie, is that you?" he asked incredulously, and she remembered that he'd never seen her cry. Very few people ever had.

She fought to control her voice. "It's me. I...I've just had an awful blowup with Curry. Could you...I shouldn't ask you to come here after what he said last night, but..."

"Give me five minutes," Jim said curtly. "He's welcome to try to throw me off the place if he wants to."

The line went dead. With tears still in her eyes, Eleanor sat down at her vanity table and tried to do something about her face. What she saw in the mirror made her angry. The same owlish face, the same screwed-up bun of hair, the same pale and lifeless look. It made her hungry for the different person she'd been last night, when men looked at her and smiled. She'd never known what it was to be admired before, and she found that it was like a drug. She put her mother's scoldings in the back of her mind and went to work.

She tore the pins out of her long hair and let it fall around her shoulders, brushing it vigorously until it began to shine and bounce back in perfect waves. She took off the unsightly glasses and put them aside. She fixed her face with a hint of makeup, the way she had for her date with Jim.

Then, riffling through her closet for something that looked leisurely, she found a patterned green skirt with a solid green terry top that just matched her eyes, and changed into them.

She slipped her feet into a pair of white sandals and went downstairs to wait for Jim, all traces of tears removed, her heart pounding hard because she was unsure of herself, of what she'd say if Curry...

Before she could finish the thought, the door to his den opened and he walked out into the hall, his face hard and lined, his stride uncompromising. She stood there like a slender young statue, dreading the confrontation she knew was yet to come.

Just then, he looked up and saw her, frozen there against the banister, and an expression she'd never seen before swept across his arrogant face.

He looked at her as if he'd never seen her before, at the slender young body whose gentle curves were no longer hidden in shapeless dresses, at the waving dark hair flowing around her shoulders, the green eyes so pale and wide that looked back at him like those of a frightened kitten.

"My God," he whispered in a voice that barely carried to her ears.

She'd never seen Curry shaken, not in all the time she'd worked for him, but he was shaken now. It puzzled her. It even frightened her a little. Her hand clenched on the banister as all the hurtful things he'd said came flooding back all at once.

"Jim's coming for me," she said in a strained voice. "I...I'll make up my time, later," she added unsteadily, "but I've got to go somewhere...." She bit her lip to stem the tears rising in her eyes.

"Eleanor..." he began hesitantly. His eyes glittered over her again, like quicksilver. "I didn't mean what I said to you," he growled, as if the words came hard, and she knew they did. "God knows, I never meant to... Will you come in here and sit down? I've got to talk to you."

She swallowed down the hurt in her throat. "There's nothing left to say," she whispered huskily. "You've already said it all."

"It was you with Black last night, wasn't it?" he asked suddenly. His eyes narrowed as they traced her young face. "I knew there was something familiar about that ramrod-straight little back, but I couldn't place it. My God, why the camouflage all these years? What was it for, Jadebud?" he demanded.

She stiffened at the familiar nickname as she recalled what he'd told Jim last night. "What do you want, Mr. Matherson? Or is it just to…keep my efficiency up?" she added bitterly.

Realization clouded his eyes and he scowled. "You heard every damned word, didn't you?"

"As you say, every damned word," she bit off. "You might tell Mandy I appreciate her taking up for me. She's better than you deserve."

"No doubt," he said quietly, and still he watched her, as if he'd never seen her before. "You never answered me. Why the disguise all this time?"

"You know what my mother was like," she said bitterly. "I don't have to remind you what she thought of painted women who flaunted their bodies. But last night was special, and Jim asked me to... I did it for him because..."

"Never mind," he said curtly. "I can guess. So that's why you're going to work for him. The little girl's got a crush," he sneered, making it sound like a sin. "My God, he's old enough to be your father!"

"You're nearly old enough to be Amanda's!" she returned fiercely.

"There's a difference..."

"I'll bet there is," she retorted, her eyes contemptuous. "If I slept with Jim, there'd be a difference there, too."

"You little tramp!"

She raised her hand and moved forward, but he caught her wrist in a steely grasp before she could connect with his firm, arrogant jaw.

Her pale eyes blazed at him like chips of Colombian emerald. "Don't you ever call me that again," she whispered furiously. "I may deserve some names, but I don't deserve that one, and you keep your foul mouth to yourself, Mr. Matherson!"

His eyes flashed at the green glitter of her own, at the little figure so tense and battle-ready, defying him, and he almost smiled. "You little hellcat," he breathed. "Do you really think you're up to fighting me?"

Something in the way he said it, in the look he was bending down at her, made her go trembly inside.

"I...I'm not afraid of you and a dozen like you!" she said with false bravado.

His darkening eyes dropped to her mouth. "Yes, you are," he murmured. "You were afraid of me the first day you came here. You still are."

"Words don't frighten me, Mr. Matherson," she replied tightly.

"You aren't afraid of anything I might say, or my temper," he agreed. "But," his voice dropped, low and caressing, "you're terrified of me in a physical sense. Or didn't you think I could feel you trembling, Eleanor?"

With a start, she realized that she was, and her cheeks blistered red. With a cry, she tore away from him, and he let her escape, standing there like some proud conqueror, confidence glittering out of his eyes as he pinned her with them.

What might have happened then, she never knew, because the sound of a car purring up the driveway claimed their attention. Eleanor turned and went quickly out the door with Curry right behind her. Jim got out of his big Buick and faced the taller man, his eyes blazing.

"I'm taking Norie out for the day," he told Curry flatly. "If you've got any objections, I'll be glad to listen."

Curry glanced back. "I told you last night that I didn't want you near this spread!" he said in a low, dangerous tone.

"Then I'll send one of the hands after her from now on," Jim replied, "but until she works out her notice, I'll see her every damned day if I want to."

"Then you'd better send one of your boys," Curry replied hotly, "because I'll have you shot if you drive through the gate!"

Eleanor gaped at her boss, barely able to believe what she'd just heard. She'd never seen Curry in such a temper before, nor had she ever heard him make an irrational threat.

"What's the matter, Curry?" Jim probed sharply. "Jealous?"

Curry's eyes caught fire and burned. Eleanor got in the car and slammed the door, her eyes pleading with Jim to let it go before something violent happened. She didn't recognize Curry in this strange mood, and she was afraid of his unpredictability.

"Jim, let's go, let's go now, all right?" she pleaded softly.

With insolent slowness, he slid in beside her. She didn't dare look at Curry as they drove away.

Halfway down the long driveway she breathed a sigh of relief. "I didn't think I was going to get away with it for a minute there. I've never seen him like that!"

"Because he gets his own way most of the time," he said tightly. "Not this time, though. Don't let him put the pressure on you, Norie. He's so damned underhanded, I wouldn't put anything past him."

"Curry's not..."

"He's dangerous," he repeated. "I don't think he'd ever hurt you physically, but we both know what his temper's already done to you. Just take it slow and easy, all right? Don't press your luck."

Eleanor wasn't sure that she believed

him, but she nodded to be agreeable. She was too tired to argue.

"Norie," he said gently, catching her eyes as she glanced toward him, "what did he say to you?"

She shifted uncomfortably and gazed out the window instead of looking at him. "Too much, and I'd rather not talk about it now, okay?"

"Sure, hon," he agreed quietly. "If you'd rather not go back at all..."

"I would, but I gave my word, Jim." She sighed. "I can't go back on it, no matter how much I might like to. It's not my way."

"Stubborn little Texas mule," he chuckled. "Tough as old boots, aren't you?"

On the outside, at least, she thought, but she laughed anyway and saw the light come back into his grim face.

They rode around looking at crops for a while—it was one of Jim's favorite pastimes, and Eleanor enjoyed the feel of the

big car as it took the bumps almost im-
perceptibly. She felt good as she looked
out at the green young cotton and peanuts
scattered over miles and miles of flat land
spreading out into the horizon. She loved
this land, from its cities to its bastions of
history. It was in her blood like a silver
thread.

It was almost dark when Jim took her
back to his ranch, the Rolling B, and ush-
ered her into the sprawling one story
frame house. His thirteen-year-old son,
Jeff, was sitting at the kitchen table with
Jim's sister, Maude, who doubled as
housekeeper and looked as if she could
outdo any two men with her big frame
and piercing dark eyes.

"About time you got back, we've been
waiting supper," Maude told Jim with a
sly wink at Eleanor. "Sit down, both of
you, and we'll dig in."

Jim sat down grimly and picked up his
napkin. He said grace with a strange curt-
ness and started to fill his plate with

mashed potatoes, steak, green beans, tomato slices and fresh corn.

"Last time I saw him look like that," Maude observed, "Ned King had outbid him for a black stallion he had his heart set on."

"It's my fault," Eleanor explained. "I had an awful fight with Curry and he rescued me."

"About time." Maude grinned. "I'm proud of you."

Eleanor blinked at her. "Why?" she asked bluntly.

"You've been letting that man walk all over you ever since I first met you. It's time he found another carpet. That Amanda person ought to do nicely," she added tartly.

"You had a fight with Curry?" Jeff asked excitedly, and Eleanor noted with a smile that he had his father's dark eyes and prominent nose.

"I did," Eleanor admitted.

The boy's eyes widened. "Did you paste him one?"

"Jeff!" Maude scolded.

"Well, I just wanted to know, I never saw anybody hit Curry who didn't end up with his nose rearranged." Jeff laughed.

"Boys!" Maude burst out. She paused, peered curiously at Eleanor, and leaned forward. "*Did* you hit him?"

"No, but I tried to," Eleanor admitted with a tiny grin.

"I wanted to hang one on him, myself," Jim broke in, as he swallowed down a gulp of his iced tea. "Damned, hard-headed bull! He ordered me off the place and threatened to shoot me if I ever set foot on it again."

Maude's eyes popped. "Curry Matherson said that? The man's sick! I've never known him to threaten anyone!"

"Oh, we've had our rivalries," Jim admitted, "but it was always friendly until now. You know, I think he's jealous of me taking Eleanor out. He acts like she's his personal property."

Eleanor blushed furiously. "He just

hates not getting his own way," she protested.

"You didn't see the way he was looking at you when you got into my car," Jim countered. "I did. I know that look in a man's eyes, and I don't like it in Curry's. He's too damned underhanded when he wants something, and right now, he's got his mind set on keeping you. God only knows what he might do...."

"I can take care of myself," Eleanor returned.

"Like Bambi," Jim growled, and his big, dark eyes narrowed as they looked into hers. "Curry's dangerous."

"I promise you he won't poison me," she said with a half smile.

"Poison is the least of my worries. Norie, we're friends, aren't we? Then from one friend to another, get out while you can. Let me go get your bags...."

"Jim," she said, stopping him midsentence. "You're my friend, and I appreciate your concern. But I promised to work out a two week notice, and I'm going to do it if it kills me. I'm not afraid of Curry.''

''I'm afraid for you,'' he persisted. ''You're just a babe in the woods.''

Her pale green eyes fixed on him. ''You're serious, aren't you? But, Jim, you can't possibly think...after all, he's engaged to Amanda.''

''Curry? Engaged?'' Maude broke in. ''He must want that redheaded scarecrow pretty bad to marry her.''

''Watch what you say in front of the boy,'' Jim growled.

''Why? He's almost fourteen,'' Maude replied, ''and he probably already knows more than you want him to.''

''Curry's fond of Mandy,'' Eleanor said, taking up for the girl.

''But he doesn't love her,'' Maude came back hotly. ''I've heard him say a hundred times that he'd never let any woman tangle up his heart the way his mother tangled his father's. The old man killed himself when his wife divorced him, you know.''

Eleanor nodded, sipping at her tea. ''It's something he's never talked about.''

''Probably because it hurt too bad. No, miss,'' Maude said with set lips, ''you'll never see Curry in love with a woman. But if he wanted one bad enough and couldn't get her any other way, he'd marry her. And don't you think that redheaded hussy doesn't know it! She's got about as much place on a ranch as I have in Saks Fifth Avenue!''

''Doing what, scrubbing floors?'' Jim teased. ''By the way, did Anderson call me back about that auction over in Alabama?''

And with the shifting of conversation, Eleanor was able to sit back and relax and stop thinking about her incorrigible boss. For the time being, anyway. And she dreaded going back to the ranch more with every second that passed.

Four

She stayed at the ranch with Jim and his family until late, and when Jim suggested that they stop by the local disco for a drink, she was all eagerness.

The music was loud and throbbing and made her bones go weak. Around them people were laughing and enjoying themselves, and Eleanor felt some of their gaiety chasing her grimness away. She'd never had more than a sherry before, but she persuaded Jim, against his better judgment, to buy her her first whiskey sour. The strong taste and smell of it was dampening at first but she found that the more she drank of it, the better she liked it. Her face began to brighten up. Her muscles began to feel loose. And all at once, all her cares and worries dissolved into music and laughter.

By the time they left the bar, Eleanor was singing the "Yellow Rose of Texas" at the top of her lungs.

She was still going strong when they reached the ranch house. Jim pulled up in front of the two-story white structure, with its lights blazing ominously.

"Eleanor, I can't let you go in there like this," Jim said grimly.

"Sure you can!" she exclaimed with a hiccup and a smile. She struggled with the door handle and spilled out into the night with a little laugh. "Oh, I'm *soooo* relaxed!" she told him.

He got out, too, and, taking her arm,

escorted her up the steps onto the porch, just as Curry came out the door. His silver eyes were blazing, his hair was rumpled by his restless fingers, his tie was off, his shirt was unbuttoned—he was the picture of impatient waiting.

"It's about damned well time you got home," he growled at Eleanor, who grinned at him.

"She wanted a whiskey sour," Jim explained wearily. "I never should have…"

"Hell, no, you never should," Curry cut at him. "Did you bring her straight here?"

Jim's lips compressed. "One more remark like that and I'll deck you!" he said flatly.

Curry reached out to take Eleanor by the arm. "I'll have Bessie look after her," he said. "Don't let your engine get cold."

Jim glared at him. "Lose your shotgun?" he challenged quietly.

Curry took a deep breath and his eyes narrowed. ''We both know you got to her in a moment of weakness or she'd never have agreed to leave me. Don't expect any favors. And I wouldn't make any dates with her, she's going to be damned busy for the next two weeks,'' he added meaningfully.

''All the same,'' Jim replied with a cool smile, ''If she calls me to come after her, I'll come, and you can damned well do your worst. Good night.''

Without a word, Curry pulled Eleanor into the house and slammed the door behind them.

Eleanor pulled weakly against the lean brown hand that was strangling her wrist as Curry dragged her up the stairs.

''Let me go!'' she protested, coming out of the stupor the unfamiliar alcohol had caused.

''When I get you sober,'' he agreed curtly. ''You're going to get a bath, little girl.''

"I had a bath already," she replied haughtily.

"Not the kind you're about to get. Bessie?" he called loudly. When there was no answer, he yelled louder, "Bessie!"

"I'm coming, I'm coming, I only have two legs and I'm using both of them as fast as I can!" Bessie grumbled as she ambled up the stairs behind them, finally catching up in Eleanor's blue and white bedroom.

"Lord, what's the matter with her?" she burst out, when she got the first look at the younger woman's tousled hair and glazed eyes. "She don't look like Eleanor. Where's her glasses? Her clothes look... Are you sure that's Eleanor?" she asked in a low, curious voice. "Where'd you find her?"

"Crawling out of Jim Black's car like a misbehaving pup," Curry said gruffly. "Put her in a cold tub and get her sober," he added with a malicious glance at

Eleanor, who was hanging onto a bedpost for dear life and glaring at him.

"But the poor child will freeze!" Bessie protested.

"If you don't do it," he said with a flash of intent in his silvery eyes, "I will!"

"Of all the unconventional things!" Bessie caught Eleanor by the arms and shuffled her off toward the bathroom. "Come on, child, I'll save you."

"Couldn't you save me," Eleanor asked dizzily, "without the cold bath?"

Bessie only laughed. "You know Mr. Curry doesn't make threats. Besides, it'll all be over in just a few minutes and I'll tuck you in and bring you some aspirin and a cup of nice, hot chocolate."

"What," Eleanor mumbled, as Bessie started unzipping the terry top, "do I need aspirins for?"

By the time Bessie got her numb body into a gown and into bed, she knew with painful clarity what the aspirins were for.

Her head was throbbing and she felt vaguely nauseated just at the thought of the whiskey she'd put away. She knew without being told that she really was going to hate herself in the morning.

Curry came in just as Bessie went out, after leaving hot chocolate and aspirin by Eleanor's bedside. He leaned nonchalantly against a bedpost to stare at the white-faced little ghost in the big bed, her black hair swirling untidily around her shoulders.

"Feel bad?" he chided with a straight face, but his silver eyes sparkled with amusement.

"I feel terrible," she said in a whisper, managing to take a sip or two of hot chocolate. She felt dizzy, and sick, and her head pounded.

"How about another whiskey sour?" he asked.

She glared at him with narrowed green eyes. "I hate you," she said levelly.

"Why? I didn't get you drunk."

"Neither did Jim, so don't you blame him," she told him.

"Why, baby?" he asked quietly.

She glanced up at his dark, somber face, and let her eyes fall to the white coverlet. "Do I need a reason?"

"I think so. I've never seen you drink before." He jammed both hands in his pockets. "Was it what I said to you, Eleanor?" he asked, his eyes darkening. "God knows, I've got a hair trigger temper, but I never meant to say those things to you. Damn it," he growled, running a hand through his dark hair, "I don't want you to go! There's no reason in the world why you can't stay on, even after Mandy and I get married! The two of you like each other."

Men, she thought, miserably, were the densest substance God ever created.

"I'd still rather go," she said stubbornly. "Jim needs me more than you do, now."

His eyes narrowed even more, dangerously glittering. "What for? To do his typing, or to…"

"Don't you say it, Curry Matherson!" she dared, knowing what would have come if she hadn't interrupted him.

"You little prude," he taunted, his eyes studying her slender body outlined under the bedclothes. "Hasn't the relationship progressed to that stage yet? My God, how has he been able to keep from dragging you off into the woods? The way you look with your hair down like that, and those ridiculous glasses off…" He frowned. "Or is all that sensuality just on the outside?"

She blushed at the look in his eyes. He made her feel threatened, uncomfortable.

"Why did you threaten to shoot him?" she asked.

He shook his head. "I don't know," he said honestly.

She dodged his piercing eyes and took her aspirins, swallowing them down with the sweet, rich hot chocolate.

"Stay, Eleanor," he said quietly, his hands jammed into his pockets.

She looked up. "I can't," she said simply. "Not after what I heard you say. I'd never be able to forget it. Not when I know what you really think of me," she added in a pained, husky young voice.

"Do you know?" he asked, and there was something dark and quiet and unfamiliar in his eyes. "Do I?"

She felt a kind of electricity burn between them as she noticed for the first time that the coverlet had slipped down to reveal the wealth of bare, silky skin where the thin spaghetti straps of her pink nightgown clung to the soft curves of her breasts. His eyes had traced those straps down, and he was looking at her in a way he never had before—a look so adult and masculine that it made her fingers tremble as they jerked the coverlet back up.

He met her shocked eyes levelly. A slow, sensuous smile tugged at his mouth and the glitter of his eyes made her feel vulnerable and weak. He laughed softly.

"You lovely little creature," he mused.

She bristled. "I thought I was a chicken," she said curtly, remembering.

He shouldered away from the bedpost nonchalantly and paused with his hand on the doorknob to look back at her. "Baby chicks are soft and downy and sweet to touch," he observed, grinning at the quick, hot color that poured into her face as he went out and closed the door behind him.

She puzzled over the remark, over the look he'd given her for a long time before she finally slept. It was just as Jim had said, Curry wanted his own way and he wouldn't stop at anything to get what he wanted. He might try flirting, or even something more to keep Eleanor from leaving. She shuddered, remembering that dark, strange flame in the eyes that had traced her body, and wondered if she could resist Curry, loving him as she did. If he ever touched her... She put the disturbing thought out of her mind and rolled over.

She overslept for the first time in three years, and ran downstairs to see if Bessie had kept anything out for her.

"Think I'd let you go hungry because you didn't wake up?" Bessie teased. She took a covered plate out of the oven and put it in front of Eleanor where she sat sipping her hot coffee at the kitchen table. "Here. Saved you some sausage and eggs and grits. Want a hot biscuit to go with it?"

"Yes, please." She looked up at the older woman sheepishly. "My head hurts."

"No doubt. Tied one on, did you?" Bessie teased.

"Not exactly. I just wanted to see what a whiskey sour tasted like."

"Found out, didn't you?" she laughed.

"Boss gone out to the field?" she queried.

"No, he's waiting for you to get yourself together enough to take some dictation," came a disapproving voice from behind her.

She flinched visibly as Curry came into the kitchen, wearing his jeans with a blue checkered work shirt half unbuttoned. He poured himself a cup of black coffee and sat down next to Eleanor at the table.

His eyes traced what he could see above the table of her trim figure in a white knit shirt and matching slacks. Her hair was left loose because she didn't have time to put it up, and her glasses were pushed casually on top of her head, giving her a sporty look.

"Looks young, doesn't she?" Bessie smiled, nodding toward Eleanor as she set a plate of hot biscuits and some jam on the table.

"Like springtime," Curry agreed. His eyes were warm on Eleanor's slightly flushed face. "Jim's influence, no doubt," he added with a contempt he didn't try to disguise.

"No doubt," Eleanor agreed sweetly, reaching for a biscuit.

His eyes flashed at her. He leaned back in the chair, sipping his coffee, and she braced herself for a storm, because it was building in his eyes.

Bessie must have felt it, too, because she dried her hands on a dishcloth, muttered something about dusting the flowers, and made a dive for the back porch.

"I meant what I said," Curry told her quietly. "I don't want Black on this property again."

"Or you're going to shoot him?" she asked carelessly, darting a nonchalant glance at him.

"I don't have to shoot him," he said quietly. "If you're determined to walk out on me, there's a lot of work I need to get through before you pack, and that won't leave much time for socializing."

His jaw set and locked. "You can save your plans for when you're on his time. I'm not paying you to play."

Her own eyes narrowed. She glanced back at him. "Since when," she demanded, "have I ever shirked my responsibilities?"

"Since you got yourself tangled up with Jim Black!" he returned.

"I'm not tangled up with him!"

His eyes lanced over her contemptuously. "Aren't you?" he asked insinuatingly.

Her face went dark with anger. She wadded up her napkin and threw it down next to the plate with her half-eaten breakfast, and stood up. "If you'd like to get started, Mr. Matherson?"

"Sit down," he said quietly, "and finish your breakfast. I won't have you passing out from hunger. You're too damned thin as it is."

She tossed back her long, waving hair. "From all my socializing, you know," she shot back. "And I've lost my appetite, thanks to you."

"Keep pushing," he said softly, rising, "and you're going to find out just how far I'll let you go."

"I'm not afraid of you," she said defiantly, turning to leave the room.

"Yet," he said as he followed her out, and the hard spoken word had an ominous sound.

They worked in a strained silence for the next hour. He leaned back in his chair at the desk and dictated letter after letter while Eleanor pretended a calm she didn't feel and managed just barely to keep up with his ruthless, deliberate speed. Every once in a while, she'd feel his eyes studying her, watching to see if he was getting her rattled. It was new, fighting Curry like this. Exciting, but very unnerving. The old comradeship had disappeared forever. Overnight they were adversaries, it seemed.

"Got that?" he shot at her when he finished the last letter.

"Yes," she replied sweetly. "Disappointed?"

His jaw clenched. His face hardened, and he started to rise with a hint of violence that made her heart leap when the door opened suddenly and Amanda breezed in wearing a jaunty gray pantsuit with a white silk blouse.

"Good morning, darling." She smiled at Curry. "Hi, Eleanor!" she added pleasantly.

"Good morning," Eleanor replied, lowering her gaze as Amanda slid her thin arms around Curry's towering neck and reached up to kiss him.

"Eleanor?" Amanda turned abruptly, her eyes wide and disbelieving as they fixed on the young girl who sat in the dowdy spinster's place at the table beside Curry's huge desk. "Is it you?" she whispered.

"It is," Curry smiled maliciously. His

eyes narrowed on his secretary's face. "Jim's handiwork," he added.

Something in Amanda relaxed at the words. "Romance in the air?" she teased.

"Maybe," Eleanor agreed cautiously.

Curry turned away. "Let me make a phone call and I'll take you down to the corral with me and show you how we brand the cattle."

Eleanor could have sworn Amanda's complexion went two shades lighter.

"Branding? But, Curry, darling," she purred, following him to place a pleading slender hand on his hard muscled arm. "I had my heart set on driving into Houston today."

"We'll go later," Curry told her inflexibly. "I can't take the time this morning. You know what we go through with roundup."

"No I don't, actually, and I'm not at all sure I want to learn." Amanda laughed nervously. "I don't like all that dust, and, darling, cattle smell so."

Curry's jaw clenched hard. "You'll get used to it."

Amanda looked resigned. "Perhaps. At least, after we're married, I can go to Houston and get away from it," she teased. "I'll keep my apartment and we can spend weekends there."

Curry didn't say anything, but his dark face was stormy. He dialed a number and waited. "Terry? I'm going to need you this afternoon if you can make it. I've got a new shipment of heifers and I want them all checked before I turn them in with the herd. You can? Thanks. See you about one."

He hung up, and Eleanor knew immediately that he'd been talking to Terry Briant, the local vet. She smiled. Terry was a confirmed bachelor, a little crusty around the edges, but he knew his job and he was well liked in the community. He'd come for Curry, but this was one of the busiest times of the year for him, and he wouldn't have made room for many people in his schedule.

"All right," Curry told Amanda, grabbing up his battered wide-brimmed ranch hat and propelled her out the door. He didn't bother to spare a glance for Eleanor, a deliberate omission that cut her. Curry could be the very devil when he wasn't getting things the way he wanted them. And, Eleanor thought doggedly, this was one time he wasn't going to win, no matter how hard he put on the pressure.

For the next two days, Eleanor did her job with robotlike precision, ignoring Curry's temper and impatience with a stoic calm that she was far from feeling. It was on the third day that things seemed to come to a head.

It had been a long day, and Eleanor was sitting in the porch swing with the phone in her lap talking to Jim Black when Curry came in from the fields where he'd been checking on the haying.

"Jim, I've got to go now," she said as Curry came up the steps.

"When am I going to see you?" Jim asked pointedly.

"Maybe this weekend. I'll phone you. Good night." She hung up before he could answer and got up long enough to put the phone back on the table by the settee before she curled back up in the porch swing.

Curry paused on the edge of the porch, leaning against one of the white columns to light a cigarette. He pushed the hat back away from his dark face and studied her through glittering eyes. The subdued light from the single fixture farther down the porch gave him a faintly satanic look. He looked as if it had been an unusually hard day. His shirt was completely unbuttoned and dark with sweat stains. His khakis were stained with grass and dirt. There was a cut on the back of one lean brown hand where blood had dried. And his face was heavily lined. He looked every year of his age.

"Talking to Jim?" he asked carelessly.

"I am allowed to do that, I suppose?" she asked sweetly.

He glared at her. "When you're on your own time," he agreed. "Did you finish those letters I dictated?"

"Every last one," she said cheerfully. "I did the production reports on the new additions, too."

"So efficient, Miss Perrie," he drawled with underlying sarcasm. "How will I live without you?"

"You could live without anybody," she said quietly. "You're as self-sufficient as a Marine."

"I was a Marine, little girl," he reminded her.

"Poor Amanda," she murmured. "She'll never really feel needed at all."

"She'll feel needed, all right," he said in a caressing undertone, and with a smile full of meaning.

She flushed uncomfortably. "No doubt," she said curtly, "but will it be enough?"

He laughed deeply. "Don't you know the answer to that?"

It was a losing battle, and she knew it. She rocked the swing into motion, turning her attention to the dark silhouette of the trees in the yard, the insistent chirp of the crickets.

"Mr. King called today, by the way," she said carelessly. "He said the plans for your new office complex had been completed by the architect and were ready for approval."

"Has Magins signed the property transfer?" he asked.

"Of course," she replied.

His eyes narrowed as he took a long draw from his cigarette. "You never cared for my tactics, did you, honey? But they work. No man ever got anywhere in big business without being just a little ruthless."

"I can't picture Jim being that way," she said quietly. And it was true, she couldn't. He was a gentleman, a caring man. Worlds away from Curry.

"He'll never amount to a damn, either," he said harshly. "That spread will never be any bigger than it is right now because he doesn't have the ambition to grow. He'll live comfortably, but he won't have much to show for his investments."

"Good for Jim," she flashed, defending him. "It's nice to find a man now and again who's satisfied with what he's got!"

"Just what has he got, Eleanor?" he asked quietly. "Charm? Sophistication? Personality? Or is he just good in bed?"

She'd never felt such rage in her life. She trembled with it as she got out of the swing and walked past Curry toward the screen door.

"I won't take that kind of insult from you or anyone else," she said icily. "You aren't going to grind your heel into me."

His lean hand shot out suddenly, grasping her upper arm so hard that she could feel it bruising, and jerked her around. She felt the heat of his body at his nearness, smelled the fragrance of tobacco mingled with the masculine odor of sweat as he held her there under his glittering eyes.

"You're getting damned sassy, little girl, and I don't like it," he said in a voice that cut. "You may stab Black with that sharp little tongue, but don't think you can get away with it here. Nobody backtalks me, not on my land."

"Oh, no, they wouldn't dare," she returned, even though the effort to talk was choking her. "Mr. God Almighty Matherson doesn't take anything from anybody!"

"As you're about to find out," he said ominously. The half-smoked cigarette went flying out into the yard, and both lean, steely arms went around her slender body, crushing her softness against the length of him.

Five

The sudden, unexpected contact made her panic, and she fought him, struggling to put distance between them, to escape those arms that felt like steel bands, the crush of his chest hurting her.

"Let me go!" she cried wildly.

"Make me," he said in a voice she couldn't recognize.

She threw her head back and looked up at him defiantly, her pale eyes throwing off sparks as she panted with the unsuccessful effort to free herself. Her body felt like metal, stiff and icy, in the first brutal embrace she'd ever endured.

"Did you expect to win?" he demanded, and his eyes burned with suppressed fury. "I could break your young body like a matchstick."

"All right, I'll admit that you're physically superior," she panted angrily, "now will you let go of me?"

"Not until I give you what you've been begging for ever since I came up those steps," he said in a low, dangerous voice.

Before she could ask him what he meant, his head lowered and she felt the crush of a man's lips against her mouth for the first time in her young life.

She stiffened at the hard, moist contact, at the urgent way he was trying to force her lips apart under the warmth of his, at the brutal way he was holding her so that she felt powerless against anything he might do.

He was making no allowances at all for her innocence, her inexperience. He was kissing her with a violent passion, his tongue running along the edge of her trembling mouth, his teeth nipping sensuously at her lower lip as his hands slid down her back to her hips and arched her against him.

A frightened moan broke from her throat. She pushed against his massive chest with all her might, feeling with a sense of terror the cool bare flesh with its light covering of curling hair against her fingers.

He tore his mouth away suddenly and looked straight into her wide, shocked eyes, dark with the fear she was feeling. Her face had gone white and even as he looked at her he felt the shudder race down the length of her body pressed so intimately against his.

The truth registered with a flash in his silvery eyes. ''My God, you've never been kissed before!'' he exclaimed, as if he couldn't believe what he was saying.

Her lips trembled as she tried to speak. "No, I haven't," she whispered shakenly, "and if...if that's how it feels, I never want to again!"

His arms loosened and she took advantage of the momentary reprieve to tear loose and run. She didn't stop until she reached the safety of her room.

All through the long night, she lived that kiss over and over again. The first time should have had something of tenderness in it, consideration. She'd dreamed of kissing Curry, of being kissed by him, but that brutal assault was more of a nightmare than a dream.

He'd meant it as a punishment, and that was what it had been. A way to show her how weak she was, how vulnerable she was to his strength. She'd learned the lesson, but in a way that became more painful with every passing second. What had he thought of her? That she was easy, that she was really Jim Black's woman? Her eyes closed on the harsh memory.

Perhaps he had thought that, until he kissed her. A man with Curry's experience would hardly mistake a novice's reaction to his passion. She remembered with a tremor just how expert his demanding mouth had been. She wondered what it would have been like if she'd relaxed against his hard body and let him teach her how it could be between a man and a woman. But playing tutor to an inexperienced girl wasn't in Curry's line, and pleasuring her had been the last thing on his mind. He had Amanda for pleasure, and Eleanor, temporarily, for business.

The only thing that didn't make sense was why he'd chosen that particular way to get back at her. Curry wasn't the kind of man to experiment, or amuse himself with an unsophisticated woman. And it wasn't his usual method of revenge, either. But Eleanor had never fought with him until the past few days. She'd always given in with a smile and gone along with whatever ruthless plan he devised with that brilliant, innovative mind of his. Now, things were different. She was fighting back, and he didn't like it, and he was using the only weapons he had.

She turned her face into the pillow, feeling its coolness drain some of the heat out of her face. Why couldn't she have fallen in love with Jim Black? He was so much more her type; gentle and kind and caring. Not at all like Curry. Curry would burn a woman alive and leave her in ashes. It was his nature. And now, more than ever, she prayed that the last days of her employment would go quickly, before he had a chance to wound her even more.

He was already out on the ranch when she finished breakfast and went to work the next morning. It was as if he couldn't face her—a ridiculous thought which she promptly dismissed. Curry never backed away from a confrontation of any kind, and he wouldn't be the least bit embarrassed or self-conscious about what he'd done last night. Before he was through, he'd even find a way to make it look as if she'd tempted him to do it.

Amanda came by unexpectedly at lunch time, looking for Curry.

"He promised to drive me into Houston today." The model pouted when Eleanor said she hadn't heard from her boss. "I'd been looking forward to lunch in a nice, quiet restaurant."

"Bessie never minds setting another place, you know," Eleanor said with kindness in her voice as she smiled at Amanda.

Amanda smiled back, her eyes puzzled at the change in Curry's secretary. "You look so different," she said involuntarily. "Younger, more alive. Is Curry right, are you interested in Jim Black?"

Eleanor shifted uncomfortably. "He's a very nice man," she admitted. "And a lot of fun to be with."

"A lot older than you, though," Amanda probed.

"He's only thirty-four," she reminded the redhead. "A year younger than Curry Matherson."

Amanda frowned. "You never call him Curry, do you? It's always his full name, or Mr. Matherson."

She shrugged with a smile. "He's my boss. I'd feel terribly uncomfortable calling him by his first name."

Amanda shook her head. "How you could work with him year after year and keep it strictly business is beyond me," Amanda said as she perched herself on the edge of Curry's desk and lit a cigarette with long, tapered fingers. "Or is that why you wore that awful disguise, to keep things businesslike?"

That rankled, but Eleanor let it pass. "My upbringing didn't allow for frivolity of any kind," she said. "But when Jim asked me to dress up for him..."

Amanda smiled with what looked like relief. "You couldn't resist, I suppose."

She laughed. "Curry said that was you with Jim the night we were in the club. How awful for you to have to sit there and hear what Curry said about you."

"It was...pretty awful," she agreed quietly. "Thanks for defending me, anyway."

"My pleasure, men can be such beasts. Is that," she probed further, "why you gave him notice?"

"Part of it was. We had a terrible argument the next morning," she admitted. "He...he said some pretty rough things about me. I suppose, added to what I'd overheard, it was really the last straw. And Jim's been trying to get me over to his place for over a year. I finally gave in."

"He has a son," Amanda said.

"Jeff. He's thirteen, and the image of his dad," she laughed. "And Maude, Jim's sister, keeps house for them. She's quite a lady."

"Sounds like a ready-made family,"

Amanda remarked. She took a draw from her cigarette and blew smoke out of her perfect, red mouth. "Children are the one problem I'm going to have with Curry. I can't risk a pregnancy for quite a few years if I'm to go on working, and I can't give up modeling. I've worked too hard, too long, to get where I am."

"You're very good at it," Eleanor said genuinely.

Amanda smiled lazily. "It's demanding, and it gets rough, but I love every second of it."

"You couldn't take time off for a baby?" Eleanor asked.

"Babies give me goose bumps," the model said drily. "I'm twenty-five, you know. And I've only got a few years left in modeling before the wrinkles start to show too much. Diapers and tears are a poor trade for spotlights and the salary I draw. Curry will understand. We'll both have to make a few compromises, but it won't be a bad marriage."

Curry didn't make compromises, but apparently Amanda hadn't found that out, yet. Eleanor had a feeling she would before very much longer.

"You must love him very much." Eleanor smiled.

"Love, my child, is highly overrated." Amanda laughed. "I'm fond of Curry, but I want him more than I love him. And he wants me. And," she added with narrowed eyes, "the day he puts the right ring on my finger, he'll get me; not before." Her gaze flicked to Eleanor's stunned face. "Shocked, darling? It's the only way any woman's going to land Curry. He isn't the love-forever-after kind. He's a virile, sensuous man who wants a woman to match that volcanic passion of his. I've held him off so far, but it won't take much longer, and I'll have him in the palm of my hand."

"You make it sound...cold." Eleanor frowned.

Amanda shook her head. "It isn't. I'll

give Curry everything he wants, and in my own way, I'll care about him. But he doesn't really need a loving, possessive wife—he's too damned independent. He needs a woman in his bed occasionally who'll leave him alone the rest of the time, and I can give him that. Very few women could live with him on those terms, and you know it. A woman who loved him would literally smother him to death. I won't.''

Grudgingly, Eleanor had to admit that the model was right. Curry wouldn't like possession, or being clung to, or depended on. He was so independent himself that he wouldn't want a woman who wasn't the same way. The thought made her sad. It wasn't really much of a future.

''Oh, darling, there you are!'' Amanda said suddenly, crushing out her cigarette as Curry came into the den, freshly showered, his hair still damp. He looked like a fashion plate in the gray suit that just matched his eyes. ''I thought you'd forgotten,'' Amanda teased, hugging him.

"I don't forget much, baby," he said with a half smile. He glanced toward Eleanor, who was avoiding his eyes with a vengeance.

"Have you got enough to keep you busy until I get back from Houston?" Curry asked Eleanor with an edge on his voice.

"Of course," came the calm reply. Still she wouldn't meet his eyes, feeling her heart running wild just at the sound of his voice as she remembered unpleasantly the last time she'd heard it.

"If you run out of work, you can start updating the files, cleaning out old material," he added gruffly. "I'll want to start fresh when I replace you."

"Yes, sir," she said deliberately, her voice quiet, unhurried, efficient.

She could feel the smouldering anger before she flashed a glance at his face and saw it there. Her eyes fell back to the calendar she was studying.

"Do I have any appointments this afternoon?" he asked.

"No. You have an 8:30 appointment in the morning with that feed salesman from Atlanta," she reminded him.

"Cancel it," he told her. "I won't be back. Tell him I've solved my feed allotment problem by trading around with some of the other ranchers, and I won't need any extra shipments."

"What if I can't find him?" she asked irritably.

"Then, you have breakfast with him, honey, and explain the situation," he said with icy patience. "Wear your glasses and one of those damned sack dresses—it'll thrill him."

Her jaw set and if Amanda hadn't been standing there, she'd have told him in no uncertain terms just where to go. He seemed to read the thought in her spitting green eyes and raised his head arrogantly, slitting his eyes down at her as if he was silently daring her to say it.

"I might just do that," she said sweetly. "I need the practice."

The emphasis on that last word wasn't lost on him, and he looked strangely uncomfortable for an instant before his hard face went impassive again.

"Let's get on the road, baby," he told Amanda, sliding a possessive arm around her tiny waist. "It's a long drive."

"Not the way you drive." Amanda laughed. "Bye, Eleanor."

"Bye," came the soft reply. She almost added a bitter "have fun," but she was a little afraid to push Curry any further. His temper was suddenly unpredictable, and Jim's words came back to her with blunt meaning. Curry was dangerous, all right, and even if she had been a little afraid of him before, it was without any substantial reason. Now, it wasn't, and she wondered how she was going to live through the next few days.

At least he wouldn't be in until late tomorrow; that was something of a reprieve. But he'd be with Amanda, and the thought of them together made her want to cry. In just a little while he'd be married, and there'd be a barrier between them that nothing could break. Tears glimmered in her pale eyes. Three years of loving him, only to lose him to a woman who could only give him passion. He'd never have the son he craved, or anyone to care about him if he got sick, or when he grew old, or...

She wiped away the tears. It was none of her business anymore. She had a life of her own to pursue, and it was, she told herself, time to get on with it. She had to make plans. She had to map out a life for herself. And it was going to take some doing to decide if Jim Black was at the end of her path, or if she needed to put more than ten miles between herself and Curry Matherson.

Jim called late that afternoon and asked her out to supper at the ranch.

"Oh, I'd love to," she agreed with a smile. "Curry took Amanda to Houston and they won't be back until tomorrow.

A whole night and day of blessed peace!''

"Are things that bad over there?'' Jim asked suddenly, and in her mind she could see the set of his square jaw and the darkness in his eyes.

She took a deep breath. ''Just about,'' she admitted finally.

''I'll be over in an hour and a half,'' he told her. ''It'll take that long to scrub off the mud.''

''Mud?'' she queried.

He chuckled softly. ''Remember that sorry old Brahma bull of mine I've been trying to pawn off on the rodeo boys?''

''How could I forget him?'' She laughed.

''Well, I finally convinced Bubba Morris that he could shed any rider who was fool enough to climb up on his back, so I was throwing a rope on him while the boys got the trailer back up to the corral.''

''There was a mudhole,'' she guessed.

"From last night's rain," he agreed.

"And the bull pulled harder than you did."

"Lady, you read my mind. Never fear, the headache's gone now, and I hope some mean-tempered cowboy rips his gut open for him."

"Sadist," she teased.

"What did Curry take Amanda all the way to Houston for?" he asked suddenly.

"Lunch."

"Why didn't they go to San Antone; it's closer," he said, abbreviating the name of the well-known Texas city affectionately, because, it was said every Texan had two homes—his own and San Antonio.

"I don't know," Eleanor told him. "I guess she wanted to look in on her apartment or something. She's been staying with a friend for the past two weeks, over in Victoria."

"Bad time for Curry to be away from the ranch, what with roundup coming on," Jim remarked. "He's got a hell of a lot of work ahead of him. It's no easy thing to move that many cattle from winter to summer pasture, and brand them, and check them, and spray them..."

"Don't tell me, I know all too well," Eleanor sighed. "Whose shoulder do you think they cry on when Curry's out of earshot? Sixteen hour days, no time off, hurting feet, no booze because Curry won't let them drink on roundup, machinery breaking down...I've heard it all, and I will again. But I understand Curry to say it was already going on; he invited Amanda down to watch the branding."

"Of those new ones he just bought, probably," Jim reminded her. "I'll bet he called Terry over to check them and give them their shots at the same time."

"That's right, he did," she replied. "Oh, gosh, I knew things were going too smoothly. I've got to live through roundup before I get out of here!"

"If we broke your leg, you wouldn't

be any more use to him,'' he said thoughtfully.

"Oh, no,'' she returned. "I need both legs to keep out of his way!''

"What's he been up to, Norie?'' he asked darkly.

"Just his usual incorrigible temper,'' she lied calmly. "I'd better get off this thing and get dressed. Want to go back to the club tonight and give the lady another charge?'' She grinned.

He paused. "Why not? Let her see what she's missing.'' He chuckled.

Jim was more outgoing than usual, and Eleanor found herself laughing as she hadn't in weeks. The club was crowded, but not so much so that she couldn't see Jim's pretty blonde shooting curious glances their way.

"She's hooked,'' Eleanor told Jim, darting a glance toward the blonde two tables over. "I'm getting vicious green-eyed looks.''

"You don't mind?'' he asked quietly.

Both narrow eyebrows went up, and she smiled. "If I did, would I be here?"

He smiled back. His dark eyes twinkled. "Isn't she a dream, Norie?" he asked.

"Now, Jim, I'm not that interested in girls," she told him.

"Oh, hell, you know what I mean!"

She laughed. "Yes, she is a dream. For heaven's sake, why don't you ask her out? Are you afraid of her?"

He shifted restlessly in his chair. "I guess maybe I am, a little." He sighed. "I'm not a young man any more, Norie, and I've got a son. There are a lot of women who'd mind that combination."

"And a lot more who wouldn't." She leaned forward. "I dare you."

"Norie, I can't."

"I double dog dare you."

"But, I...."

"I double-double dog dare you."

He threw down his napkin. "That does it, no man alive could refuse a double-

double dog dare! But if I come back bleeding, it'll be your fault.''

"I'll put on the tourniquet,'' she promised faithfully.

She watched him out of the corner of her eye as he walked up to the table where the fragile looking blonde was sitting alone and bent over to speak to her. She saw the look on the girl's face, and something inside her relaxed. That beaming, tender look the blonde was giving Jim said more than a volume. Eleanor smiled involuntarily and turned her attention back to her supper.

All Jim talked about on the way back to the ranch was Elaine and how sweet she was and how amazing his luck was that she'd finally agreed to go out with him.

"And what do you mean, finally,'' Eleanor chuckled. "You never asked her before, you big old shy maverick.''

"Thanks, Norie.'' He sighed. "You'll never know...''

"Yes, I do,'' she protested, "and

you're very welcome. What are friends for?''

''To help each other, it looks like.'' He pulled up in front of the ranch house and switched off the engine. ''I only wish there was some way I could help you besides giving you a job.''

''I'm fine, Jim, really,'' she said, twisting her purse in her hands. ''Just…a little worn, and time will fix that. I may not stay with you for a long time, you know,'' she added gently. ''I'm not sure where I want to go yet. I've never given any thought to a future beyond this place,'' she said, gesturing toward the Matherson property. ''Now, I have to decide what I want to do with my life. You know, I've only just realized that there are things beside ranch work that I could do. I could work for lawyers, or doctors, or I could go back to school. I could even train for an entirely new profession—go to a technical school, or train on the job. The world is opening up for me.''

"It won't bother you to leave here?" he asked shrewdly.

She looked down at her darkened lap. "I didn't say that. But time heals most wounds, even the kind Curry Matherson dishes out. I'll live. People do."

He tilted her face up to his eyes in the dim light that came from the front porch.

"Curry's a damned fool," he said quietly. "Amanda will never make the kind of wife he needs. She'll be sick of the ranch in two weeks, and back to Houston to recuperate. Unless I miss my guess, she'll live there and leave Curry here and he'll have to come to Houston just to get to see her. She'll never adapt."

She shrugged. "He loves her," she said simply.

"No, he doesn't. He wants her, which is something you'd have to be a man to understand. It's a kind of burning thirst that usually gets quenched after one good sip. But she'll keep him hanging until the ring's on her finger, and then it'll be too late to go back.'' He sighed. ''Curry's not the kind of man to back out of a deal once he's given his word. That includes marriage. No, he'll stick it out. He's too bullheaded to cry quits.''

''It won't be much of a life, will it, Jim?'' she asked softly.

''No, hon, it won't. But don't think you can tell him that.''

She laughed mirthlessly. ''When was the last time *you* tried to tell him something?'' she challenged.

''I remember it well, as it happens. It was 1969, and I warned him that if he bought that damned helicopter to use to herd cattle, he'd spend more time maintaining it than he would flying it.''

''That was before my time,'' Eleanor said. ''What happened?''

''One of his temporary summer hands got smashed at a local bar and decided to take the thing up at midnight one night.''

''Could he fly a helicopter?'' Eleanor asked.

"Well, as a matter of fact, he'd only been in one twice. He knew how to start it and how to get it in the air. The only problem," he added with a grin, "was that he didn't know how to get it down. Hit a pine tree, broke off a blade, and came down in the lake. My God, you should have seen Curry when they told him. He hasn't let a drop of alcohol on the place during roundup since. And," he added with a grin, "he's never bought another chopper."

"So that's why he uses the little Cessna," Eleanor remarked.

"That and the old-time ways. They're really better on some ranches." He chuckled.

Eleanor sighed. "Well, I guess I'd better call it a night. It's been such fun, Jim. Thank you."

"Thank you," he said with a smile. "If Curry gives you a hard time, come on over, and hang working out your notice. The Blacks will take care of you good and proper."

"The Blacks," she returned, "are super people—all three of them."

"Now, if you'll help me convince Elaine of that…"

"Any time," she promised. "Good night."

"Good night, Norie."

She went into the house with a dreamy smile, relaxed because Curry wasn't home, content to be alone and decide what she was going to do with herself when the job ended. It wasn't going to be so bad after all. Once she got over the initial jolt of not waking up to see Curry at the breakfast table in the morning, in his den during the hours he had to be inside, on the porch late in the evening when the world was still….

Six

As she moved through the halls, the grandfather clock chimed twice in a loud, metallic voice. She hadn't realized that it was so late. She'd really enjoyed herself tonight as much from playing cupid as from Jim's company. She had a feeling that Elaine was going to be good for the lonely widower and his family.

"What the hell do you mean coming in at this hour of the morning?" came a loud, angry voice from the doorway of the den.

She froze for an instant, not expecting that, as she tried to decide whether or not she was hearing things. She turned slowly to find Curry leaning against the door, his hair tousled, his eyes glittering like sun on a knife blade, his whole appearance threatening and dark.

"I...we were at the club," she faltered. "I thought you were in Houston. You said..."

"You don't even look kissed, little girl," he growled, and his eyes dropped to her mouth with its soft traces of lipstick, her hair flowing in soft waves around her shoulders, looking as neat as if she'd just left to go out. "I always suspected he was something of a cold fish. Lida Mae started running around on him barely a year after they were married."

"You don't have any right to talk that way about him," she replied coldly.

"Why not? I'll bet he's been giving

me hell behind my back ever since he started taking you out.''

Before she could deny it, the flush on her high cheekbones gave her away.

''Come have a drink with me, Jadebud,'' he said gently, shouldering away from the door facing with a weariness that was so alien it was faintly shocking. ''I've had a hell of a night.''

She followed him hesitantly into the den and watched him fill two glasses with whiskey and ice, lacing one liberally with water to weaken it. He handed her the weaker drink.

''Sit down,'' he said, indicating the sofa.

She perched herself on its edge, trying not to cringe when he dropped down beside her and crossed his long legs. The pale brown slacks he wore emphasized the powerful contours of his thighs and he was wearing a cream silk shirt that was partially unbuttoned, and since he never bothered with an undershirt, it left a wide expanse of bronzed chest and curling dark hair uncovered. He looked unbearably adult and masculine, and the sensuality that clung to him like the exotic cologne he wore made her feel like running.

"Don't start tensing up on me," he said roughly, darting a quick glance at her rigid profile. "I've learned my lesson, and I don't have the patience to initiate terrified little virgins into the intricacies of lovemaking. You're perfectly safe, so you can lean back and stop looking like a fawn in the hunter's sights. I won't rape you."

She went red as a beet and sipped at her drink, hating him now as she'd loved him before, wishing she had the sophistication to fight back.

He studied her quietly and a heavy, bitter sigh left him. His lean hand brushed away a thick swathe of hair from her cheek with a tenderness that puzzled her.

"I'm in a hell of a temper. I didn't

mean to say that, little girl." He set his drink down and lit a cigarette. "I feel like I've had the floor cut out from under my feet tonight."

She studied her drink, aching with conflicting emotions. "Do you want to talk about it?"

He took a long draw from the cigarette and exhaled a cloud of silvery smoke that almost matched his eyes. "Amanda wants to live in Houston," he said simply.

"She's a top model, Mr. Matherson, her job..."

"Don't call me that!" he said curtly, his eyes pinning her.

"You...you are my boss, what else should I call you?"

"My name is Curry."

She turned her head away from that penetrating gaze, but his hand caught her under the chin and turned her right back to face him.

"My name," he repeated in a low, deep tone, "is Curry."

She swallowed nervously and bit at her lower lip. "All right."

"Well, say it!"

"Curry," she said in a hesitant, frightened tone. She didn't recognize him in this strange mood.

"That's better." He let go and leaned back again, flicking ashes into the ashtray he'd set on the other side of him on the sofa.

"Anyway," she persisted, "you know how much her job means, she's worked very hard to make it as far as she has."

His eyes narrowed, glittered, as they met Eleanor's. "I want a son," he said stubbornly. "At least one, maybe two or three. I want a woman who's here when I need her, who puts me first. I don't want a glossy photograph, Jadebud, I want a flesh and blood woman who'll burn like hellfire in my arms when I make love to her, who'll make sons with me!"

She turned every color of red in the spectrum, feeling herself charred with embarrassment.

"I'm sorry," he said curtly. "I forget sometimes how unworldly you really are, for all that you've spent the past three years in an earthy environment. I've spent my whole life here, and I don't find anything embarrassing or shocking about procreation. It's a natural, beautiful part of living. But you wouldn't know about that, would you, not with a mother as icy as yours was."

"Leave my mother out of this! You don't have the right to sit in judgment on her; no one does."

"After what she did to you?" he demanded, meeting her hot gaze levelly. "My God, it was like kissing a rock, Eleanor!"

She turned her face away from him, remembering with clarity those few painful seconds in his arms when she felt his mouth demanding impossible things of hers. "I'd like to forget that ever happened," she whispered unsteadily.

"Do you freeze up on Black like that?" he asked quietly.

"He doesn't kiss me," she said before she thought about it.

"He what?" he asked sharply.

"I told you before, he's my friend, not my lover, and what right have you got to pry into my life?" she demanded.

He shifted, turning so that one long arm rested across the back of the sofa, and his eyes burned where they touched her.

"Not much, I suppose," he admitted. He ran a lean, brown hand through his tousled hair, and watching it, she wondered how that thick, charcoal-colored hair would feel under her fingers.

"I've been rough on you this week," he said without malice. "I don't even know why, but I seem to want to hurt you lately. Maybe it's for the best that you do go. I've never had a complaint about your work, Eleanor, if that's any consolation. I couldn't have asked for a better secretary."

"Thank you," she said demurely, lowering her eyes to her glass as she took another sip of the fiery liquid. It was beginning to relax her a little and she sighed as she rocked the glass so that the ice clinked.

She made a pattern in the condensation on the cool surface of the squatty container. "Is that all that's wrong with you?" she asked after a minute. "That Mandy doesn't want to live on the ranch?"

He took another deep, harsh breath. "She's trying to move up the wedding," he admitted. "We never discussed a definite date, but now she's pushing for next month. I'll be damned if I like being pushed!"

"She loves you," she said, hurting inside even as she defended the redhead. "Naturally, she's..."

"That isn't it. Something's not right about this whole damned thing, and I'm wearing out my mind trying to figure it. She tried to seduce me tonight," he said frankly. "And she damned near succeeded. I'm so hot-blooded, it was all I could do to get out the door."

"Please, you shouldn't be telling me this...." she protested.

"I've got to tell somebody, damn it, who else is there?" He clenched his fingers around the glass and leaned forward, staring blankly ahead. "I don't know what kind of game she's playing, but I don't like it. She's always said 'no' before. Now, all of a sudden, anything goes. It looks very much as if she wants a guarantee. And she knows I'd never turn back if there was the risk of a child."

She got up and moved to the bar, reaching idly for the whiskey bottle.

"What's the matter, little saint, can't you even discuss adult subjects without trying to climb into an alcoholic haze?" he shot at her.

She froze with her hands on the bottle. "It embarrasses me, if you must know," she said in a choked voice.

"You should have entered a convent, then. How old are you now?" he asked gruffly.

"Almost twenty-one."

There was a long pause. "Twenty?" he asked incredulously.

"I'd just turned eighteen when you hired me," she reminded him.

"You always seemed so much older...but that was part of the disguise, too, wasn't it?" he asked bitterly. "You're young with Black, like a filly just feeling her legs. Yet with me, there's something matronly about you, a kind of reserve...even when I took your mouth that night, you turned to stone against me. And I hurt you, didn't I?" he asked with a strange, sweet tenderness in his deep voice. "I bruised you all over because I couldn't make you give in. Not a very satisfactory introduction to passion, was it, Jadebud?"

She felt a shudder run the length of her body as he brought it all back again. "I didn't know...men got like that," she admitted weakly. "I...I thought the first time it was gentle."

"The first time is usually with a boy your own age who'd be afraid to touch you," he replied quietly. "And, yes, it's usually gentle. But a man...kissing is something entirely different for a man, Eleanor. A tightly closed little mouth becomes a challenge; he needs to taste a woman, not just feel the softness of her mouth against his. It's damned hard to explain," he said finally and with soft laughter. "I suppose it all goes back to the basics, to passion. A man my age likes to arouse a woman more than he likes to simply kiss her, because it usually ends up in a bed. That's one reason I never take out a woman who doesn't already know the score. Until Amanda came along," he added gruffly. "And by the time I realized how innocent she was, I was hooked."

"I still think it will work out," she

said in a soothing tone, turning to look at him. He wanted the woman, and if he loved her, all Eleanor wanted for him was to see him happy.

He met her soft gaze and his silvery eyes studied her for a long time, from her face to her slender body and back up again. "You're lovely, little girl," he said softly. "As lovely as a dream, and I can't think of anything I'd like better than to draw you down with me on this sofa and teach you how to make love."

She felt her eyes going wide with fear as she set the glass down quickly. He'd had too much to drink, apparently, and she didn't feel like being a stand-in for the woman he really wanted.

"I...I'm very tired," she said quickly, moving toward the door. "And sleepy. And I've got a lot to do tomorrow."

"Afraid of me, Eleanor?" he asked patiently.

She turned at the door, her whole look puzzled and uncertain. "I'm terrified of you, Curry, and that's God's own truth,'' she admitted. ''Please don't make it any harder for me. I don't want to be used, like a toy to amuse you when Amanda's not around. I don't want to be flirted with. I'm your secretary and you're my boss, and if it's going to be any other way than that, then please let me go now. I can't bear being played with,'' she finished on a pained whisper.

''Honey,'' he said quietly, ''what makes you think I'm playing?''

She whirled and left him sitting there, feeling her heart bursting against her ribs as she made her way quickly up the stairs. And when she finally got into her room and ready for bed, that last gentle question kept her awake for another hour despite the fact that her senses were exhausted.

He was at the breakfast table when she went down only hours later, her eyes still bloodshot from lack of sleep, and she wondered idly why he hadn't gone out with the hands.

His pale eyes shivered over her as she sat down across from him, and a hint of a smile curved his mouth.

"It's about time you crawled out of bed," he told her, sipping his coffee as he eyed her. "I want you to come out with me today."

She stared at him uncertainly. "Where?" she asked.

"Roundup starts this morning."

"Oh!" She couldn't hide the surge of excitement that statement created. Every year she'd begged to be taken along when the first of the cattle were brought in from winter pasture to be moved to summer quarters. New calves were branded, and the vet was around to check for disease. It was the most exciting time of the year on a cattle ranch.

"You love it, don't you?" he asked with narrowed eyes. "Every bit of it, from the branding to the culling, even tossing hay to the horses. Yes, Miss Priss—'' he nodded at her start of surprise ''—I hear what goes on around here. You conned Johnny into letting you feed the horses in the stalls. Or didn't you think he'd tell me?''

''I thought ranch managers were supposed to keep their mouths shut,'' she grumbled.

''They are—but you're forgetting, I don't keep a ranch manager, I keep an assistant manager. Nobody manages this spread except me,'' he added.

''As if I didn't know.'' She sighed. ''You manage everybody on it, too, when they'll let you.''

''You used to let me,'' he said.

''I grew up,'' she said smugly.

''Not quite,'' he said with a meaningful lift of his eyebrow.

She glared at him across the table. ''Maybe it depends on the man, did you ever think of that?''

The smile got deeper. ''Or maybe the

man just didn't try hard enough. Next time, I won't be so impatient.''

Her eyes widened and she dropped them to her plate with volcanic eruptions taking place in her blood. ''There won't be a next time,'' she said firmly, although her voice wasn't quite steady.

''Are you coming with me? You'll have to change. That pretty pantsuit will be ruined if you wear it.''

She glanced down at the white slacks and matching top. ''More likely it'd turn red,'' she mused. ''Jeans and a cotton shirt okay, boss?''

He smiled at her. ''And boots. Got yours?''

''Of course. I do ride, you know,'' she reminded him.

''I haven't seen you on a horse in two months.''

''You haven't looked in six months to see what I was on,'' she teased.

He didn't smile at that. His pale eyes caught hers and held them for a long time with a searching look that made her forget the blistering heat of the cup in her hand.

Bessie came in noisily with the coffeepot and broke the spell. Eleanor held her cup out with a smile while she fought to calm her stampeding pulse.

"Haven't touched your breakfast," the housekeeper scolded. "He ruining your appetite?" she nodded toward Curry.

"Maybe it's the other way around." Curry grinned, winking at Bessie.

"Well, aren't we in a good mood this morning!" Bessie said brightly as she filled his cup again. "What'd you do, foreclose on somebody?"

"You," he told the buxom woman, "are pushing your luck."

"Not likely. Who'd you find with the gumption to put up with you?" she shot back.

Eleanor smiled. "She does have a point," she put in.

"Look who's talking," Bessie scoffed.

"You only just got the good sense to leave after three years of it."

The smile faded as Bessie went out again, and she felt an aching emptiness inside her that breakfast couldn't fill.

"Don't think about it," Curry said suddenly, his jaw set, his eyes somber. "Let's take it one day at a time, honey."

"I'm still going, Curry," she told him gently.

He met her eyes. "We'll see."

"*We* won't see anything," she returned, putting the cup down. "I'm not taking any more orders, and you're not going to bulldoze over me...oh!"

He'd moved out of his chair while she was in midsentence to stand by her chair. All at once his head bent, and he pressed a hard, quick kiss against her open mouth.

"Stop talking and get your clothes changed," he told her. His lean hand ruffled her hair. "I can't wait all day."

He was gone out the door before she

could come up with a lucid sentence. Her fingers went involuntarily to her parted mouth. She could still feel the warm, hard pressure against them.

He was on the phone downstairs when she got changed into faded jeans, boots, and a blue-patterned cotton blouse. She'd tied her hair back with a blue ribbon to keep it out of her face and left off her makeup. The prospect of spending a whole day with Curry had been too tempting to turn down, but when she heard him call Amanda's name while he spoke into the receiver, all the color went out of the day for her.

"I told you," he was saying gruffly, "I'm not being railroaded, Amanda. Either we wait until I'm ready, or we call the whole damned thing off. You don't want to? Then what the hell are you doing in Houston?" There was a pause and he cursed under his breath. "You couldn't turn it down? Then stay there. Don't 'oh, Curry' me! I want you like hell, but not enough to let you lead me around like a broken stallion. My terms, Amanda. No ifs, buts or maybes. My terms, or nothing. All right.'' He sighed roughly. ''Maybe the breathing space will do us both good. I'll see you in two weeks, and we'll talk about it. Sure. Bye.''

He hung up and stood there staring down at the phone, his hard-muscled body as taut as a stretched rope, running a restless hand through his hair. He looked as if he might explode, and Eleanor hesitated uncertainly on the bottom stair.

As if he sensed her presence, he turned, and his pale, troubled eyes looked full into hers.

''Problems?'' she asked softly.

He nodded. His eyes traced her slenderness like an artist's brush. ''Take your hair down,'' he said.

''It gets in my eyes,'' she faltered.

He moved close, and his lean, brown

hands reached up to untie the ribbon, letting the soft waves tumble down. His fingers tangled in the softness gently, touching the warm flesh of her throat through it, his breath coming harder and heavy at her forehead.

"Please," she whispered shakily as his fingers contracted bringing her face up to his suddenly blazing eyes. "Please don't use me to keep your mind off her," she whispered.

His jaw clenched, his nostrils flared. "Is that what you think?"

"It's what I know. I...I couldn't help overhearing." She dropped her eyes, licking her dry lips as she fought to keep her emotional upheaval from showing. "I'm sorry you're upset, but hurting me won't help."

"Would it hurt you?" he asked softly.

She didn't know what he meant, but she was afraid to ask. "Shouldn't we go?"

"Norie, don't be afraid of me," he

whispered against her temple, using the familiar nickname for the first time. "Little Dresden china doll, I won't hurt you again, physically or emotionally. Don't run from me."

"I...I'm not running, I just don't want..."

"Don't want what?" he murmured, placing his lips against her closed eyelids. "Let me make love to you."

"No!" She pushed away with all her strength and backed against the wall like a stalked fawn, her pale green eyes enormous in her pale face.

His eyes narrowed painfully. "God, don't look like that!" he exploded.

"You...you make me feel like something hunted," she exclaimed. "Please!"

He whirled with a hard sigh and a muffled curse, running his hand around his neck tightly as if there was an ache in it he couldn't ease.

"Come on, if you're not afraid to ride with me," he growled as he reached for his battered work hat and started out the door.

She followed along behind him, the day ruined, afraid of him as she'd never been. She hesitated on the bottom step as he swung into the pickup and threw the passenger door open for her.

"Well?" he shot at her.

She got in, slamming the door firmly. She couldn't look at him.

"Is it Black? I'd just like to know."

She shifted restlessly, staring at the dash unseeingly. "No," she replied.

"My God, it's like trying to pry a clam open," he grumbled as he started the truck. "All right, forget it!" he said, and accelerated out of the yard.

Seven

In a stoic silence, Curry drove down to the twin barns where his horses were kept. His face was set, and a cigarette burned forgotten between his fingers. He was so unfamiliar like this, she thought. The old days of friendly banter seemed to be gone forever, leaving only cold silence or anger between him and Eleanor.

She stared at the lush green pastures stretching to the horizon. The river was just visible in rare glimpses through the hardwoods that ran along its banks. Both of the truck's windows were rolled down because Curry didn't bother with air-conditioning options in work trucks, and it was blazing hot. She missed the ribbon that would have kept her hair out of her face, and blushed when she remembered how she'd lost it.

Curry unknotted the bandanna around his throat and handed it to her. "Tie your hair back with that," he said, as if he'd read the thought in her mind. "It's hot as hell out here."

"Thanks," she murmured. She drew the weight of her hair behind her neck and tied it with a double knot, letting the ends stream down. The bandanna smelled of Curry's tart after-shave, and she knew she'd never give it back. It would go into her jewelry box with all the other tiny mementos of him that she'd accumulated over the years; things to be taken out only rarely in the future and looked at through tears while she tried to get used to a world that he wasn't in.

"We'll pick up the horses on the way," he said as he lit a cigarette. "Sure you're up to this, baby?" he added with a half smile. "It isn't pretty."

"I'm not a satin doll, Mr. Matherson," she replied, stung by the sarcasm in his deep voice. "It won't be the first time I've seen cattle branded and castrated."

"No, it won't, will it?" He frowned thoughtfully, handling the pickup easily with one hand as he took it over the rocky pasture and Eleanor bumped and bounced in her seat as it absorbed the rough terrain on its shocks.

"Were you hoping I'd pass out from the heat?" she asked, peeking at him from her long eyelashes.

His eyes flashed over her young face. "Flirting with me, Miss Perrie?" he mused.

She shifted pertly in her seat and looked out the window, her heart throbbing. "Me? I wouldn't dream of such a thing, Mr. Matherson," she replied in her best businesslike tone.

He laughed softly. "Brat."

"Male chauvinist," she countered, loving the easy atmosphere that was reminiscent of earlier, more companionable times.

"Me?" Both dark eyebrows went up as he glanced at her. "Honey, I'm one hundred percent in favor of women's liberation."

"You are?" she asked suspiciously.

He took a long draw from the cigarette. "Dead right. I think we ought to liberate women from housework so they'll have more time to wait on us."

"Incorrigible man!"

His eyes glittered over her soft curves with a familiarity that raised her blood pressure two points.

She moved restlessly. "Would you mind not looking at me like that?" she asked uneasily.

"Yes, I would."

"Curry!" she groaned, his name slipping from her tongue as if she'd always used it.

"That's the first time you've ever said that," he remarked with a quick glance into her eyes. "I like the sound of it."

"It slipped out," she replied tightly.

"My God, do we really need the post-mortems?" he growled. "You make me feel sixty when you call me 'Mr. Matherson.' I'm not that much older than you are."

"Fourteen years," she reminded him.

He stopped the truck in the middle of a rise and let it idle, turning toward her with one long, lean arm across the back of the seat while he studied her thoughtfully. "Does it bother you that much?" he asked.

The look in his silvery eyes did, but she couldn't give him the satisfaction of knowing that. She dropped her gaze to the leather seat between them, to the powerful legs covered in blue denim.

"Why should it?" she asked as coolly as she could.

"Because the emotions you arouse in me lately don't have much to do with dictation," he said bluntly.

That brought her face jerking up. She gaped at him, her lips parted as her breath gasped through them.

"And now that I have your attention," he continued casually, "would you mind not trying to build fences between us for the little time I have left to enjoy the pleasure of your company?"

"I didn't realize it was a pleasure," she told him.

"Neither did I," he admitted. "But, then, we don't tend to appreciate things as much until we're faced with the loss of them, do we? I'm going to miss you one hell of a lot, little girl. I've gotten...used to you."

"You make me sound like a habit," she murmured.

"One I could acquire without a great

deal of effort,'' he replied with narrowed, considering eyes as he sat there watching her.

"I'd rather we just left it at a business relationship,'' she said through taut lips.

"Would you?'' he asked gently. "How would you know, Eleanor? I've never made love to you. Not in all that time we've been together. You don't know me in a physical sense.''

"Don't I?'' she whispered, embarrassed, remembering that night....

He drew a deep, harsh breath. "It wouldn't be like that again,'' he said gruffly. "I wouldn't hurt you.''

She studied her folded hands. "I'm not going to stay, Curry,'' she said tightly, "no matter what you say or do. You don't have to flatter my vanity. No man would be blind enough to want me, remember?'' she added bitterly.

"I said that, didn't I? My God, those horrible glasses and shapeless dresses, that staid personality that clung to you like spiderwebs—would any man have wanted you that way?''

''Probably not,'' she admitted quietly. ''Maybe that was what I wanted, I don't know. I thought what a person was inside was the most important thing, not what he or she looked like on the outside.''

''That's true, to a certain extent,'' he admitted. ''But, honey, what's on the outside is what attracts a man to look for what's on the inside, didn't you know?'' He smiled mockingly. ''A man reacts to the look, smell, taste and touch of a woman, little girl. It's the way he's made. The first thing I noticed about Amanda was the silky way her skin felt under my hands.''

Amanda. The sound of her name was enough to put the sun behind a cloud for Eleanor. ''She's very lovely,'' she admitted in a subdued tone. ''She'll come around, Curry, if you just give her a little time.''

''Eleanor,'' he asked gently, ''are you in love with Jim Black?''

She avoided those searching eyes. "I don't have to answer that."

"I'd like to know." He leaned forward to stub out his finished cigarette. "I don't want to see you hurt, in any way."

"Jim isn't the kind of man to ever hurt a woman."

His head lifted arrogantly. "And I am?" he asked narrowly.

She met his eyes bravely. "Yes," she agreed, "you are. You...you don't really like women, I don't think, except in a purely physical way. Love isn't in your book of words, is it, Curry?"

He leaned back against the door to study her. "Neither are unicorns and the tooth fairy, honey," he admitted carelessly. His pale eyes glittered with bitter memory. "You know why I feel that way, don't you?"

She nodded.

"You've never asked me about it," he remarked.

"It wasn't any of my business," she

said quietly. "I don't like prying into painful subjects."

"No, Jadebud, you don't," he said, reaching out to smooth a strand of hair away from her dusky cheeks. "I could tell you anything, do you know that? Things I could never tell anyone else. It's always been like that between us."

Her eyes avoided his. "I'm flattered that you trust me."

"Is that all it is?" he asked quietly.

She couldn't answer him, was afraid to even think he meant...

He started the truck and pressed down on the accelerator.

Later, riding over the pasture with Curry brought back childhood memories. Rocking gently on the back of the chestnut gelding he'd given her, Eleanor studied the lay of the land she'd spent her life in.

Texas was a land of contrasts, of desert and green pastures, of mountains and flatland, cattle and high-rise apartments, cattle drives and desperadoes and men in handmade Italian silk shirts.

She breathed in the sweet smell of grass and closed her eyes dreamily as the horse moved lazily and the saddle leather creaked in the bright morning sun. In her mind she could picture the old trail riders punching the herd along the Chisholm Trail, the Goodnight-Loving Trail, all the famous cattle trails that ragged, weary cowboys had followed so many years ago. It was impossible to look around and not feel the sense of history here, the ghostly presence of those rugged souls who withstood the ravages of storm and drought and Indian war parties and rustlers. It excited her to think about the proud history of the land that was her own.

"Where are you?"

Curry's deep voice broke her out of her reveries and she darted a sheepish glance toward him, towering over her on his coal black stallion.

"I was riding on the Chisholm Trail," she confessed.

He chuckled, his good humor returning under the wide canopy of sky and cloud. "You baby," he teased. "How many copies of Zane Grey did you cut your teeth on?"

"The first hundred," she replied. "I loved everything he wrote." She studied his shadowed face under the battered ranch hat he wore. "Curry, did you like Western history when you were a boy— you know, about gunslingers and lawmen and cattle drovers?"

He reined in and crossed his forearms over the pommel. After a moment, he pushed his hat back on his head and studied her in a still, waiting silence. "What made you ask that?" he mused.

She shrugged. "I don't know. I was curious." She turned her gaze back to the horizon. "How much farther is it to where you've got the cattle?"

"A mile or so. Think your backside can take it?"

"I'll live," she replied, easing up and down in the saddle. Her legs would probably feel like twin bruises tomorrow, she thought wryly.

"You're nervous today," he observed as they started moving again.

"Am I? I don't feel nervous," she assured him.

"We've never been alone like this before," he said without looking at her. "Bessie was always around, or some of the hands." He turned his head and caught her eyes. "I could drag you off into the trees and no one could hear you if you yelled your head off," he teased gently, but something dark and dangerous began to cloud his eyes as they swept over her face.

She bit her lower lip. "I'm safe, you told me so," she replied with a confidence she didn't feel. "You didn't have the patience, you said..."

He drew a sharp, angry breath. "You've got a memory like a steel trap, haven't you, Eleanor? Do you remember every damned word I've ever said to you?''

"I didn't mean to make you angry."

"Then shut up, and you won't," he said bluntly, giving the stallion its head, leaving her to follow or not as she chose.

Several hundred cattle were raising dust and a lot of noise where they were held in pens connected to a network of chutes that were used to sort them according to age, sex and breed. Two men were herding the cattle from one pen into the chute, yelling and slapping the animals on the rump with their hats to move them along. Another man was on top of the railing of the chute to keep the animals moving along. Other cowboys straddled a two-way gate that separated calves from cows and steers.

"Noisy as hell isn't it?" Curry laughed as they neared the pens. "The sorting takes a while, and this is only a fraction of the whole herd."

"Which herd is this?" Eleanor asked, shading her eyes with her hat.

"The breeding herd—some of it. We'll run them through before we even start on the grade cattle."

"I don't envy those men their jobs," she said, shaking her head. She searched the area. "I don't see Terry," she remarked, looking for the local veterinarian's tow head among those of the cowboys.

Curry glared over at her. "Isn't Black enough for you, honey? Or are you just collecting scalps as you go along?"

She wondered at the bite in his voice. "I just wondered where he was, Curry, that didn't mean I want to assault him while he vaccinates the herd!"

"He likes you," he persisted.

"Horrible glasses and all," she said with a defiant gleam in her pale eyes.

He got down off his mount with a quick, graceful motion and strode over to the corrals.

Terry Briant arrived just after the sorting was completed, while the men were preparing the branding irons. Eleanor took a place beside the chutes to watch as the calves were herded into them and chased down to the metal trough at the end of the chute and the entrance to the branding corral.

Her ears caught the mingled sounds of cows crying for their calves, calves bawling in fright, cowboys laughing and talking in a mingled potpourri of English and Spanish as they coped with the day's work.

The team at the end of that chute, which included the thin, blond-headed vet, was experienced and fascinating to watch. The calf's neck would be clamped in the trough and within one minute he'd be branded, earmarked, castrated, as most male calves were, vaccinated and tattooed—all in one smooth operation. The air was thick with smoke and dust and the smell of burning hair, but Eleanor had seen this many times before, and she didn't even flinch as she watched—which seemed to amuse Curry to no end when he glanced at her from the branding corral.

One small sick calf was separated from the rest, and Curry brought it out in his arms.

"It's going on dinner time," he told Eleanor, nodding for her to get on her horse. "We'll have a bite to eat and come back."

"All right." She mounted, taking the reins in her hand and steadying the horse as Curry handed the small calf up to her. She swung it over the saddle horn and smoothed its silky coat with a smile.

"Poor little thing," she cooed. "Going to put him in the barn until he heals?"

He didn't answer her. He was looking up into her face, one hand on the saddle horn, the other on the horse's flank, and she doubted if he'd heard a single word. He just looked at her, his eyes steady and unblinking, with an expression in them she couldn't decipher. They sparkled like diamonds, vibrant, piercing.

"Curry?" she asked softly, unaware of the picture she made with her hair just slightly windblown, her cheeks full of color, her eyes lovely in the sunlight.

"You look right at home," he remarked with a half smile. "As natural on that horse with a calf in your arms as a frontier woman might have looked a century ago."

"Frontier women," she reminded him, "were wrinkled and tough as leather and could outshoot, outdrink, and outcuss their menfolk. And besides, they got married when they were barely thirteen and had twelve kids."

"Would you like to have twelve kids?" he asked.

She looked down at him, her eyes involuntarily tracing his angular face and firm, chiseled mouth, the curve of his dark brows, the thick hair that made tiny waves at the nape of his neck. A man like Curry would have sons as tall and tough as he was, as handsome as himself.

"Green and gray," he murmured thoughtfully as he searched her eyes. "What color would their eyes be?"

"Gray," she said softly, as if she knew.

He jerked his eyes away suddenly. "Let's go."

She blushed to her heels as she realized what he'd been saying, what she'd replied... She watched him swing into the saddle, but whirled her mount before she had to look him in the eye.

They went back to the ranch house long enough to eat the thick ham sandwiches Bessie had waiting, but the silence at the table was unusual to say the least. Bessie kept glancing from one of them to the other, trying to puzzle out what was wrong.

It was almost a relief to get back to the turmoil of roundup, Eleanor thought as they made their way once again to the holding pens on fresh mounts.

The strain between Curry and Eleanor was almost tangible. Even the busy ranch hands seemed to sense it. There was an ominous feel about the afternoon as calf after cow after steer was run through the gate into the branding corral. It all went smoothly until one big, enraged Hereford bull managed to escape the men and tear his way into the branding corral without being snared.

Bill Bridges, one of the more experienced cowboys moved quickly to throw a rope on the bull, but he reckoned without the animal's frightening speed. In seconds, the rope was torn from Bridges' hand and the bull was charging at him furiously.

After that, everything seemed to happen at once. Bridges suddenly went down with the bull snorting and hooking its horns at him as he rolled frantically trying to dodge the thrusts.

Curry went over the rail like a track star, a gunny sack held in one lean hand, and started to distract the bull.

"Get him out of here!" he yelled to two of his men, who promptly jumped into the corral and dragged the white-faced cowboy out.

Curry flicked the sack at the bull, and turned to leap back over the ring, but a quick jerk of the snorting animal's head caught him in the side. Eleanor saw him grimace tightly with pain, and he went down like a crumpled bag.

Terrified, without even thinking, Eleanor slipped between the rails and ran to him, picking up the gunny sacks as she did.

"You stupid beast!" she raged at the bull, whapping it across the rump with all her strength with the sack, taking out the terror and fury she felt on it.

Distracted, the bull turned away from Curry, tossing his big head, his red and white coat wiggling with the motion as his big eyes stared at the pale young woman.

Meanwhile, the other hands dived into the corral and got to Curry, ignoring his feverish curses as he ordered them to "get that damned woman out of the corral!"

Jed Docious settled the problem by slinging a hard, wiry arm around Eleanor's slender middle and half carrying, half dragging her to safety while the others danced around to keep the bull from charging. Two other cowboys dragged Curry to safety.

Once outside the ring, Eleanor made a beeline to Curry, who was stretched out on the ground with blood oozing from the wound in his side as one of the men worked to stem the bleeding by applying pressure with a clean handkerchief.

"Are you all right?" she asked him breathlessly. She dropped to her knees pushing at a strand of gritty, damp hair as she looked down into blazing silver eyes in a face gone white under its tan.

"You hotheaded little mule," he began slowly, the whip in his voice was so sharp that it cut. "You empty-headed, idiotic, stupid little fool! You could have been killed in there, you damned lunatic!" He was warming up now, and what followed was louder, rougher, and laced with language like nothing she'd ever heard him use before. Her face had gone red and tears were rolling down her cheeks before he finally stopped to take a breath.

"Boss," Docious interrupted hesitantly, "we need to get you to the sawbones and have him patch you up before you bleed to death."

"What the hell do I need with a doctor?" Curry wanted to know, flashing his blazing glance in the tall cowboy's direction. "Get me the hell in the house and call Jake in off the fence line. He can patch me up."

"Curry, he's good at patching up animals, but..."

"Don't tell me what he is, Docious, I know damned well what he is, just get him, will you?" Curry growled. He glared up at Eleanor, whose face was white as paste. "Let Eleanor take over riding fence," he added sarcastically. "Since she's decided she's one of the hands!"

That was the last straw. She turned with a sob and ran for her horse, tears streaming down her cheeks. She rode away without a backward glance.

Eight

Eleanor stayed in her room for the rest of the day, refusing Bessie's offer to bring her supper up, doggedly refusing to even ask about Curry even though she was aching to be reassured that he was all right.

Night came, and she turned on the small lamp by her bed, taking up her seat in the armchair by the window to stare blankly out of it with eyes that burned from too many tears.

She heard the door open, and one quick glance showed her that it was Curry. She bit her lip, feeling the tears come again, warm and wet and salty, trickling into the corners of her mouth.

Curry came and knelt in front of her. His shirt was open down the front, and she could see the stark white bandage against the bronzed flesh of his rib cage, his chest with its mat of dark, curling hair. His hands went to her waist and he held her gently, looking straight into her misty eyes, his own gaze dark and quiet with what might have been pain.

"You scared the hell out of me, little girl, do you know that?" he asked softly. "I died twice watching you in the ring with that bull, knowing that any minute the horns could catch you, the way they caught me. You sweet, crazy little fool, what if he'd gored you in the stomach? You might never be able to bear children, did you even think about that?"

She bit her lip, shaking her head softly.

"I...I thought he was going...to kill you," she said simply, and her tear-filled eyes met his, shimmering like spring leaves in the rain.

"Honey," he whispered softly, "what the hell good would it do me to live if your life was the price I had to pay?"

A tear worked its way down her flushed cheek. His hands went to her cheeks, drawing her forward, and his lips sipped away the tear, following it back to her closed eyelids, his tongue gently brushing the long, wet lashes in a silent intimacy that throbbed with emotion.

"Curry?" she whispered unsteadily, her hands going involuntarily to his broad shoulders.

His breath came hard and heavy. "What?" he whispered in a voice that wasn't quite steady as his mouth began to explore, to touch and lift and taste the contours of her face.

"Are...you hurt bad?" she asked.

"I'll have a scar out of it," he murmured absently.

"You...you bled so much," she whispered. Her fingers dug into his hard shoulders as the lazy, brief caresses began to work on her like a narcotic.

"It wasn't any more than a cut and a bad bruise," he murmured. He looked into her misty eyes, searching them in a silence that burned, with an intensity like nothing she'd ever experienced. His gaze dropped to her parted lips and studied them for such a long time that her heart pounded in her chest.

"I'm going to make you want it this time," he whispered huskily. "I'm going to make you ache for it."

Before she could find the words to answer him, his mouth was brushing softly, lazily, against hers, teasing her lips apart, his whiskey-scented breath mingled with hers as his practiced mastery brought a moan from her throat.

His teeth nipped gently at her lower lip, his tongue probed the soft, tight curve of her mouth with a slow, stroking motion that made the trembling start in her untutored body.

She drew back quickly, her eyes wide with surprise as they looked directly into his. She expected to see mockery there, but there was only a vague, patient tenderness.

"It's all right," he said softly. "I'm not going to force you this time."

The tears were drying on her cheeks, the unhappiness being replaced by a wild kind of excitement as his lean hands tightened on her waist.

"I don't know very much," she murmured uneasily as her hands went to his broad shoulders and rested there.

"Forgive me, little one," he said with a slow smile, "but it shows."

She searched his pale, glittering eyes. "Curry, do men really like to kiss like that?" she asked.

"Oh, yes," he murmured, studying the puzzled little face so close to his.

"Why?" she asked.

"If you'll relax and let me do what I want to for the next minute or so, I'll show you."

She sat very still as his dark face came even closer. Her eyes closed, her breath sighed against his firm mouth as it touched and caressed and began to open, pressing her trembling lips apart with a slow, sweet, relentless pressure. She felt the intimacy of it right through her body. It made feelings stir deep inside her that she'd never felt, and as they grew and grew, her sharp nails involuntarily bit into his hard shoulders as she felt his mouth deepen the kiss to an intimacy that brought a choked moan from her throat.

"Oh, Curry!" she whispered brokenly against his mouth.

"Don't talk," he replied, in a voice she didn't recognize.

His lean hands moved under her cotton blouse to caress her bare back, and the touch was like fire. She pressed closer suddenly, her mouth hungry for his, her body blazing under the lean, sure hands that moved with an urgent pressure from her back to the silken curves of her breasts and the length of her slender body.

With a suddenness that left her hanging between paradise and reality, he tore away and stood up. He went to the window without a backward glance and drew in a harsh breath while he pulled a cigarette from his pocket and lit it.

"I didn't mean to go that far," he said finally, in a voice rough with self-contempt.

Her stunned eyes went over his long back, loving him, needing him, still burning from the fever of his ardor.

"Did I do something wrong?" she asked in a subdued tone.

"No, honey, I did." He stared out the window. "Little innocent, don't ever let a man touch you like that again unless you're willing to accept the consequences. It's too arousing."

She blushed. It embarrassed her to talk like this, to feel like this. He made her feel ashamed of her own breathless response and as the bitter words sank in, her cheeks flamed with the memory of what she'd let him do. How could she tell him that she could only have felt that kind of abandon with a man she loved? She dropped her shamed eyes to her lap.

There was a movement as he turned, and she felt the piercing gaze on the back of her neck.

"God, Eleanor, don't look like that!" he growled shortly. "You're out of the nursery!"

She jumped out of the chair and went madly toward the door, feeling like some hunted animal trying to escape the hunter's bullet.

"Baby, don't," he said in a calmer voice as her hand reached for the doorknob. "I didn't mean to snap at you."

She hesitated, hearing the soft thud of his boots on the carpet as he came up behind her and caught her by the waist, drawing her rigid back against the length of his body.

"Men get like this sometimes," he explained patiently, "when they're hungry for a woman they can't have. Call it frustration, Jadebud. I wanted you very much and because of it, I let things get out of hand. I won't let it happen again."

She relaxed a little against him, her mind fighting to cope with the upheaval of her emotions. He had her so confused, she barely knew her own name, and the newness of what she was feeling, added to the embarrassment of the liberties she'd allowed him, brought the tears back to her eyes.

He felt the sob that shook her and turned her into his arms, holding her tight against him while she cried.

"Hush," he whispered at her ear. "God, I'm sorry. I had no right to touch you like that. I'm a man, Eleanor, long past my adolescence. It's damned hard for me to accept limits, if that's any excuse. But what happened...happens between men and women,'' he added, searching for words. ''It's a very natural part of lovemaking, and nothing to be ashamed about. You're a normal, warm and responsive woman, and there's not a frigid bone in your body. And for the record, I'm damned glad I was the first.''

She buried her hot face against his chest, and he chuckled softly.

''We'll keep it low key from now on, little girl,'' he said gently. ''Come back out with me tomorrow. We'll stop by the store after we get through with the last of the breeding herd and pick up some canned sausages and soft drinks and have lunch on the river.''

''I'd like that,'' she said softly. Her fingers pressed patterns into his blue-checked shirt, feeling the warmth and hardness of his chest through the soft material.

One of his hands came down to still

the movement. "Don't tempt fate," he said quietly.

Her fingers curled into a tight ball. "I'm sorry," she said quickly.

"So am I," he murmured. "If you were a little more sophisticated, I'd strip the damned shirt off and show you how I like to be touched."

She tried to avert her face, but he caught her in time to see the slow burn on her cheeks and he grinned down at her wickedly.

"Little spring bud," he whispered. "You're a far cry from my usual kind of woman."

"So is Amanda," she reminded him quietly, feeling the hurt as she suddenly remembered that flashy diamond Curry had given his new fiancée. Fiancée!

"Is she, Norie?" he asked seriously. His eyes searched hers. "I wonder. It takes experience to try and seduce a man. I don't think you'd know how."

She averted her face. "I think it would

come naturally if a woman loved the man.''

''Amanda loves my money, all right,'' he agreed. ''But not enough to put up with the ranch twelve months of the year.'' He drew in a deep breath. ''Would you be happy several hundred miles away from a man you loved?'' he asked.

She shook her head without thinking, her soft, misty green eyes tracing every hard line of his face, lingering on his square jaw and the firm curve of his mouth.

''When you look at me like that, you're asking for trouble,'' he said in a husky voice, his hands tightening like steel bands on her slight rib cage.

Her breath came fluttering, the look in his eyes made her hungry and reckless. ''What kind of trouble?'' she whispered shakily.

He bent, lifting, curving her body into his arms as he trapped her there. ''What kind of trouble do you think, you little witch?'' he murmured as he caught her mouth roughly under his.

Nine

She felt her knees turning to water while he crushed her lips under his ruthless, hungry mouth. He lifted her slender body against his, fitting her expertly to its powerful contours. It was like being joined by gigantic magnets, she thought while she could, as if they were glued together so tightly that they could never separate again. She clung to his neck, drowning in the sensations he was causing as he kissed her, yielding completely, loving him until nothing mattered but that he never let go....

A shudder went through his tall body as he drew back, looking down at her through slitted, blazing eyes. His breath came like a runner's, hard and heavy and slightly rasping.

"Lovely little witch," he whispered in a shaken voice. "God, you learn fast!"

"Your ribs!" she remembered suddenly, her eyes dropping to the half-hidden white bandage where his lean hand pressed against the pain.

"It was worth it," he replied. He put her away from him. "I'll see you in the morning. Want some supper now? If you do, I'll have Bessie bring you a tray."

She shook her head.

His teasing eyes dropped to her mouth. "Not hungry any more?" he asked in a voice like a caress.

She shook her head again, with a smile.

He touched a finger to her swollen mouth. "Good night, honey," he murmured, and went out the door, leaving her eyes glued to the space where he'd been.

She woke up wondering if the night before had been a dream. There was no sign of bruising on her, no turmoil in the eyes that met hers in the mirror. But she felt a tingle of emotion at just the thought of meeting Curry this morning and she dressed in her jeans and a white cotton top with a feeling of vibrant anticipation.

He was at the breakfast table waiting for her when she came downstairs, and his silver eyes ate her the minute she walked through the doorway.

She flushed at the intensity of the look, surprised by the sudden inexplicable difference in their relationship. It was as if what had happened last night—and it was no dream, she read that in his eyes—had opened the floodgates, and there was no stopping the raging current they'd created.

"Did you sleep well?" he asked in a deep caressing voice when she sat down beside him.

"Yes, thank you." Her eyes darted up for an instant to meet his and dropped quickly. "Did you?"

"I'll tell you later," he murmured. He leaned over and kissed her lightly on the mouth. "You look lovely in white, little one," he added.

She smiled, feeling a warmth like summer sunlight inside her when she met his level gaze. He returned the smile, and a current of electric hunger seemed to link them for several seconds so that neither could look away.

"Well, aren't we affectionate this morning?" Bessie enthused, and broke the magic spell as she walked in with a platter of sausage, scrambled eggs and biscuits.

Curry lifted a dark eyebrow at her, not a bit perturbed. "Remind me to raise your salary in 1996."

"What makes you think I'm going to put up with you that long?" Bessie returned, leaving with a quick wink at Eleanor and a face like the cat that got the cream.

"What if I raised your salary?" Curry teased, and she could feel the laughter in his eyes. "Would you stay?"

She felt the light go out of the world, remembering, and all at once she wondered if these were some more of Curry's ruthless tactics to get his way.

Would he go so far as to court her to keep her on the ranch? She hadn't considered the possibility before, she'd been too caught up in the surge of emotion he'd created between them with those expert kisses. But the mention of her staying brought it all home with a vengeance. Curry was engaged to Amanda, for heaven's sake! That was a fact, and all the teasing kisses in the world wouldn't change it. If he'd wanted to marry Eleanor, or even been in love with her, it wouldn't have taken him three years to find out.

"Never mind," Curry said. His sharp eyes caught the freezing of her features, the stiffening of her body. "We'll take it one day at a time. Eat your breakfast, honey, I've got work to do."

"Should you be pushing so hard with that wound?" she asked, and nodded toward his ribs under the khaki shirt.

"I told you once, I'm as tough as nails," he said with a smile. "It's a little more sore today, but I don't expect to die from it."

"Stubborn man."

"It's my middle name."

She smiled, but her heart wasn't in it. She finished her breakfast quickly, already dreading being alone with him for the rest of the day. When it came to Curry, she had no resistance, and she was afraid of what he might demand of her innocence. He was dynamite at close quarters, she'd learned that already, and

the fact that she was in love with him
would make it all that much harder to resist him.

How could he do this, how could he use
her own emotions against her just to keep
her working for him? Secretaries, even
private ones, weren't that hard to come
by. Not for a man with Curry's looks and
charm. Or maybe it was just the principle
of it. That he didn't want his old rival Jim
Black to get one up on him by stealing his
very efficient secretary. Either way,
Eleanor thought miserably, she was the
one who stood to suffer because of it.

The noise and dust and heat were far
worse the second day than the first, and it
seemed to take forever to work the herd
after they were sorted.

One mean-looking heifer got her foot
stuck between the rails and it took a half
hour to free her. The men's tempers were
running hot, and Curry's was at its finest,
when lunch time finally rolled around.

Curry stomped away from the corral, dirty and drenched in sweat, his face flushed with temper, his eyes cruel.

"Let's go," he bit off, joining Eleanor where their mounts were tied.

"Was that the last of the breeding herd?" Eleanor asked.

"Almost. We've got about a hundred or so to go today." He smoked quietly on his cigarette as they rode along toward the small country store down the road. "God, I'm getting too old for this kind of aggravation."

"Jim Baylock's opening a new nursing home," Eleanor suggested. "Maybe we could get your name on the waiting list."

He glared at her through narrowed eyes. "I can't go," he told her. "The damned cattle would cry their eyes out missing me."

She grinned at him. "Only the cows," she laughed.

"Keep it up and I won't feed you."

"If you don't, I'll get weak from hunger and fall off my horse," she threatened.

He smiled at the banter, and she could actually see some of the tautness drain out of his tall body, his set face. He finished the cigarette and threw it down into the dust as they reached the old-fashioned little store with its single gas pump out front.

They bought Vienna sausages and crackers, along with soft drinks, a block of cheese, and moon pies. Loaded with their bounty, they rode down to the cool trees by the river and sprawled on the soft grass to eat.

"We'll get chiggers," Eleanor said lazily. She popped a small sausage into her mouth and savored every bite as she washed it down with an orange drink.

"You can get Bessie to rub you down with alcohol to get rid of them," Curry replied.

"I bet you never get chiggers," she observed. "Your hide's so tough they couldn't get through it."

He grinned. "So I've been told."

She finished her lunch and leaned back against the grassy bank with her arms behind her head. "It's so cool here," she murmured with closed eyes. "So quiet."

"Shangri-la, Eleanor," he agreed. He stripped off his shirt and stopped down at the edge of the river to splash cold water over his sweaty chest and shoulders and neck.

She watched him quietly, her eyes drawn to the powerful muscular body, remembering the feel and touch of it with a hunger that ached. Of all the men to fall in love with, why did it have to be one as unreachable as Curry Matherson? Why couldn't it have been Jim Black? She smiled, remembering Jim's last phone call, his enthusiasm for the little blonde. It sounded very much as if there'd be a wedding before long, and she was glad for the lonely widower. He'd been alone so much over the years, he deserved a little happiness.

Curry straightened up, tossing his shirt to the grass as he dropped lazily beside Eleanor, leaning on one elbow with his long body stretching out on the green grass.

"I love it here," she murmured, closing her eyes to savor the watery voice of the river.

"Is there anything about ranch life you don't like?" he asked with sudden bitterness.

She sighed, drinking in the delicious peace of green shadows and silvery water. "No, there isn't anything about it that I dislike. Oh I'd hate to live in a city, wouldn't you, Curry?" she asked abruptly, enthusiastically, turning to meet his silver eyes and finding a look in them that made her heart turn over. It was a sensuous, totally adult look that appraised every inch of her body, and she was more aware than ever of the masculine appeal of that broad, bronzed chest so close to her with its mat of hair still damp from the water, the bandage slightly dark where the water had just touched it.

"You're trembling, Eleanor," he said quietly. "What are you afraid of?"

"I'm not afraid of anything," she denied shakily.

His fingers slid under the sleeveless white top at her shoulders, lightly stroking the warm young flesh over her collarbone with a teasing pressure that made her tremble.

"Your skin feels like warm silk," he remarked gently. He leaned forward, easing her onto her back and trapping her there with his arms on either side of her.

"Shouldn't we get back?" she asked too quickly.

He caught her frightened eyes and held them with his. "I don't want to go back right now," he said, bending to tease her lips with his. "You don't want to, either, if you'd admit it. I need you, Eleanor...."

He drew her face up to his and kissed her gently, slowly building the pressure until he felt her mouth relax and part, until he heard the soft moan that sighed against his lips. He took her hands and spread them onto his bare, cool chest, teaching her wordlessly how to touch him, how to caress and arouse him.

His body was hard and unyielding where she touched him with slow, nervous fingers, learning the hard contours with a sense of wonder, testing the wiry strength of the dark hair on his chest with a fleeting pressure that brought a groan from the mouth that devoured hers.

She looked up into his face, seeing the passion harden it, darken his eyes as he returned her frank regard.

"God, the way you look when I love you..." he whispered huskily, sketching every soft, lovely line of her face.

"You shouldn't be," she whispered unsteadily.

"You want it," he replied flatly, with that inborn arrogance that was as much a part of him as his square, relentless jaw.

She lowered her eyes to the muscular chest under her fingers. So did he, she thought, but only as a means to an end, and she knew it. With a sigh, she rolled away from him and got up, standing under a spreading oak at the river's edge while she caught her breath.

"What's wrong?" he said from a few feet behind her.

"It's not fair, Curry," she said. Her hands fluttered as she clasped them behind her, drinking in the cool breeze that blew off the bubbling water below the bank. "Not to Amanda, not to me. You're engaged."

"I know." There was a harsh sigh, and a long pause, after which she smelled the cigarette smoke that drifted thick and pungent past her face. "Avalanches aren't that easy to stop, little girl. Once they start rolling downhill, it's next to impossible to stop them."

"Riddles?" she asked quietly.

He moved beside her to lean back

against the trunk of the mammoth tree. He'd put his shirt back on, although it was hanging open, and she could see marks on his chest where her nails had bitten into the bronzed flesh while he was kissing her....

"I want you," he said bluntly, his eyes catching the way she stiffened at the words. "I want you like hell every time I touch you, and I can't help it any more than I can help breathing. And, damn you, you want me just as much!"

She felt the trembling start in her legs and work its way up. Her eyes closed on the emotion in his deep voice, an emotion so convincing that she almost believed he felt it. But she knew Curry too well. She knew his tactics. It was just another trick, and only a fool would fall for it.

"Physical attraction fades in time," she said. "I don't want an affair with you, Curry, I don't want it with anyone. I want something permanent."

"A ring?" he growled. "Just like

every other damned woman, you'll give yourself if the price is right, is that it? I won't be owned, Eleanor. I'm as susceptible to a soft young body as the next man, but there's a limit to the price I'll pay for it."

"Aren't you buying Amanda's?" she asked bitterly, glaring at him.

He paused. "It's different with her. She doesn't want ties, and neither do I."

"You don't consider marriage a tie?" She looked straight into his glittering eyes. "Do you think I'd use the back stairs to your bedroom while she spent the better part of her life in Houston, Curry? Is that what you had in mind for me?"

He had the grace to flush, his eyes stormy and strange. "It wouldn't be like that."

"Oh, wouldn't it?" She laughed without humor. "Do you think I'm so stupefied by a few of your kisses that I'll tell Jim Black sorry and climb into your bed?

I'm sorry to disappoint you, but I'm still going. If you thought you could keep me here by blinding me with your potent charm, you lose.''

He looked for an instant as if he'd been hit from behind. ''You think that?'' he asked in an ominously quiet tone.

''Did you think you had me buffaloed?'' she replied with a coolness that was smoothly convincing. ''That I wouldn't guess what you were up to? I may be naïve, Curry, but I'm not stupid. I've seen you in action, remember, and I know better than most how low you'll stoop to get what you want. You couldn't stand letting Jim Black walk away with anything you considered your property, could you?'' She drew in a sharp breath. ''Did you have to grit your teeth when you kissed me, Curry?'' she asked bitterly. ''After all, you said yourself that no man would be blind enough to want me.''

''What the hell are you talking

about?'' he asked in a frankly dangerous
voice.

''You know what I'm talking about,
you've tried everything short of proposing
to keep me here!'' she said furiously.
''You and Jim have been rivals in business for years, and you've never taken a
challenge from him that you didn't win.
Did it really bother you that much to have
him hire me right out from under you? Or
was it just that you couldn't stand having
a woman around the place who could resist you?''

His eyes caught fire. ''Resist me?'' he
growled. ''You little wildcat, I could lay
you down in that grass and have you right
now if I wanted you, and you'd let me!
So don't stand there like some Victorian
society matron and tell me how immune
you are to me. I just might let you prove
it!''

She wrapped her arms around her chest
and turned her attention back to the water.
She didn't say another word.

"You're still the shriveled up little chicken you were before you shed your disguise, Jadebud," he growled cruelly. "For your information, I wasn't trying to get you into my bed. I thought you might benefit from a little experience if you're going to be tangling with the likes of Jim Black. But from now on, your education can go hang! If you think I'd trade Amanda for a repressed little bundle of piety like you, you're crazy as hell!"

She went white in the face. Absolutely white, her nails bit into her forearms as she fought not to let him see the effect the vicious attack had on her.

"You're free to go whenever you damned well please, Eleanor," he added curtly. "Making love to you every day is too damned high a price to pay to keep you at your desk."

She heard him walk away and a minute later, there was the creak of saddle leather and the thud of a horse's hooves dying away.

It was only then that she let the tears roll freely down her pale cheeks. She'd wanted the truth, and now she had it. Only four more days, she reminded herself, and she'd be able to walk out the door with a clean conscience. But how would she survive it? How?

Ten

____

Roundup went on, but without Eleanor. There were no more trips out to the holding pens, no more quiet rides with Curry. He avoided her like the plague, speaking to her only when it was necessary.

She was grateful for his absence. She felt wounded, and she needed time for the scars to heal.

"Something wrong between you and Curry?" Bessie asked her at supper one night when Curry was still out working on the ranch.

Eleanor stared into her plate. "Just the usual irritation," she said lightly, trying to make a joke out of it.

"Things calmed down for a little while there."

"So they did," Eleanor agreed.

"Don't want to talk about it?" the housekeeper said knowingly.

Eleanor smiled wanly and shook her head. "It's best forgotten."

"Still going over to Jim?"

"Yes, for now."

"And then?"

Eleanor shrugged. "It's a big world," she said with a short laugh. "There's no telling where I'll wind up."

"You'll write?"

She said yes, of course she would, and dug into her meal, knowing full well she wanted no more contact with the ranch, ever, once she left it. It would hurt too much.

Jim Black's phone call the next afternoon came at the best possible time. Curry's continued avoidance, and the lack of work to keep her busy, was driving her to an attack of nerves she'd never experienced before.

"How much longer?" Jim teased. "I'm getting impatient over here, and I just may need your help with a wedding before long."

"Oh, Jim, congratulations!" she enthused. "See, I told you it would work out!"

"Yes, you did, and Elaine and I will never be able to thank you enough for that 'double-double dog dare' that started it all. When, Norie?"

She swallowed. "Three more days. I wish it was tomorrow."

"What about if I talk to Curry?"

"I...I wouldn't do that," she murmured.

He drew a hard breath. "I knew I should have kept a check on you!" he grumbled. "If I hadn't been so wrapped up in my own life...hon, I'm sorry. It's been bad, hasn't it?"

The sympathy brought tears to her eyes. "Yes," she admitted unsteadily. "It has."

"Are you free the rest of the day?"

She brightened. "Yes. I've got everything out of the way that I need to do."

"Good. How about if I come get you, and you can have supper with all of us tonight? I'd like you to get to know Elaine."

She smiled. "I'd like that very much," she said genuinely.

"I'll pick you up in thirty minutes. That long enough?"

She was ready, dressed in a pale green clinging dress with her hair waving softly around her shoulders, when Curry arrived back at the ranch house just as Jim drove up.

The two men studied each other quietly. Jim was neat in a dark sports coat with matching slacks and a cream-colored shirt. Curry looked as if a whirlwind had hit him, his jeans dusty, his shirt torn and wet with sweat, his hair damp with perspiration.

"I'm taking Norie over for the evening," Jim said as if he expected an argument.

"That's your business," Curry said abruptly. His pale eyes speared the other man.

"I'm glad you finally realized it," Jim replied. "No hard feelings, Curry. I hope you'll come to the wedding."

Eleanor didn't think she'd ever forget the look on Curry's dark face when Jim told him that. Obviously he thought Jim meant Eleanor, and his jaw locked violently, his face seemed to harden to solid rock.

"Wedding?" he asked in a strange tone.

Jim grinned. "It happens to all of us sooner or later, doesn't it? I hope you and

Amanda will be as happy as we expect to.''

Curry didn't say another word. He turned, sparing Eleanor a glance so hateful she felt as if he'd struck her, and walked straight into the house without a backward glance, slamming the screen door behind him.

''What was that all about?'' Jim asked.

She sighed and shook her head. ''Beats me,'' she told him. ''If anything, he'll give a party when I leave. He's that glad to see me go.''

''Is he, now?'' Jim's eyes narrowed thoughtfully.

Eleanor got into the car and sat quietly until he started it.

''Thanks for rescuing me,'' she told him. ''Supper was going to be another ordeal.''

''What's eating him?''

''Amanda won't come and live on the ranch after they get married,'' she explained. ''He's furious. He doesn't think she cares enough to stay with him, and he's like a fire-breathing dragon lately.''

"So that's it," Jim remarked, as if he'd been thinking something very different. "I knew that wasn't going to work out. Amanda's a lovely girl, but she's not ranch stock.''

"It's more than that," Eleanor said, staring out the window as she spoke. "She doesn't love him, Jim. She's more interested in how much she'll be able to spend, and keeping up her career, than she is in taking care of Curry.''

"Does he love her?''

"Apparently," she replied, "although he says no. He wants her," she added in a subdued tone. "I suppose that's as close as he can come to feeling anything for a woman.''

"He doesn't know what he's missing." Jim grinned.

"You old maverick," she teased. "You look ten years younger. Elaine's influence, I'll bet!"

"You'd be right, too. Oh, what a girl!"

And she was. The petite little blonde, once she got over her initial reserve when she and Eleanor were introduced, turned out to have a live wire personality. There was a loveliness in her that had nothing to do with exterior beauty. She was a caring person, and everything she felt for Jim was in her eyes when she looked at him.

Maude liked her too, and it showed. Eleanor noticed that Jeff, too had been captured by that bright smile and sunny manner.

"Looks like you're not going to have to win anybody over," Eleanor teased the older girl when they were washing up the dishes after supper.

"I know," Elaine replied with a smile. "It was so strange, the way everything seemed to fall into place. I seemed to fit here the first time I walked through the door. I love Maude and Jeff, too, and I'm crazy about the ranch. Jim's teaching me how to ride.''

''You'll make a good wife,'' she told the blonde. ''He's needed someone like you for a long time. He got a raw deal with his first wife, I guess you knew that.''

Elaine nodded. ''I'll try to make it up to him.''

Eleanor grinned. ''I don't think you'll have to try too hard.''

''You're still coming to work for him, aren't you?'' Elaine asked suddenly, as if it really mattered to her. ''Jim's told me what you had to put up with over there. I hope you'll still feel welcome—I'd like very much to have someone my own age to talk to. We could go shopping together and everything.''

''If you and Jim don't mind,'' Eleanor replied, ''I'll come for a few weeks.'' She looked down at the soapy water. ''I...I don't know where I'll wind up eventually. Even ten miles away from

Curry may not be enough, I'll just have to play it by ear.''

"Do you love him that much?" Elaine asked softly.

Eleanor bit her lip. She nodded, hating the tears that misted in her eyes.

"I'm sorry it didn't work out."

She shrugged. "We don't always get everything we want in life," she said philosophically. "And sometimes there's a good reason. I'll live."

"Couldn't you come sooner?"

"I promised him two full weeks, and that's what he's going to get if it kills me. Anyway," she laughed, "it's just a couple more days. After the time I've already put in, it's going to be a piece of cake.''

Curry was waiting for her in his den when she finished breakfast the next morning, dressed in a gray business suit that matched his eyes. He spared her a grudging glance when she walked in the door.

"I've left a couple of letters on the

Dictaphone," he said in a voice like ice. "I'm going to be out of town today; you might tidy up in here so that your replacement can find things."

Your replacement. He made it sound so impersonal, as if the three years she'd spent working in this room weren't worth anything at all to him. And that was probably true. Curry wasn't sentimental. He'd tried to keep her, he'd failed, and now he wasn't even making an effort to be courteous. She'd refused his generous offer and he had no more time for her.

"Yes, sir," she said in a subdued tone.

"When's the wedding?" he asked with his back to her.

"I don't know. Soon," she said vaguely.

"You don't sound enthusiastic."

"I think it's wonderful," she corrected. "It's going to be a good marriage. One of the best."

Curry's hands jammed hard into his pockets. He drew in a deep, harsh breath.

"I'm going to bring Amanda home," he volunteered into the silence. "It's time she faced up to what marriage means. I'm not going to have my wife living one place while I live in another. She's going to understand that from the beginning."

"You don't give an inch, do you?" she asked sadly, turning away so that she didn't have to meet his eyes. "She's the one who's going to have to make all the sacrifices."

"If she loved me, giving up her career to be a mother wouldn't constitute a sacrifice, and you damned well know it!"

She did, but she wasn't going to puff up his ego by admitting it.

"Does Black want children?" he asked suddenly.

She laughed softly, remembering what Elaine had told her. "Oh, yes," she said with a smile, "a whole huge houseful of them, assorted."

There was a tense silence between them. "Damn him!" Curry breathed violently. "Damn him, and damn you, too!"

She turned, astonished by the emotion in his dark face, his blazing eyes, trying to puzzle out what in the world was wrong with him.

"Don't be here when I get back," he told her in a voice so cold it seemed to choke him. "Get your bags packed today, and get out! I never want to set eyes on you again, do you hear?"

She could only nod, strangled by the demand, her voice buried.

He spared her one last, scathing glance as he opened the door. "Good riddance," he murmured. "I've had enough puritans to last me a lifetime. I wish him joy of you."

And with that last, puzzling statement, he was gone. She stood there white-faced, half relieved that the stress was finally over, that she wouldn't have to stay here and watch him with Amanda while another part of her was already wilting like a flower suddenly thrust from full sunlight into the cool shade.

Tears were pouring down her cheeks when she put the cover on her typewriter for the last time and left the room.

Leaving was harder than Eleanor had ever imagined. It was one thing to know she was going to do it, quite another to make it an accomplished fact.

Three years was a long time to leave behind. There were so many memories in the sprawling ranch house. Nights when she and Curry sat up and watched the late show together while he dictated correspondence during the commercials. Long, lazy afternoons when he'd stop her in the middle of something and they'd go driving, or riding out to see the new calves. Periods of such comradeship that they seemed infinitely closer than boss and secretary. And now, all of it was only a memory.

Jim came to get her, bag and baggage, and Bessie cried.

"Fool man," the housekeeper sobbed, "hasn't got eyes in his head to see with! Amanda'll never satisfy him!"

"It's his life, Bessie, he has to do what he thinks is best," she replied tearfully, defending him unconsciously, as she always had.

"He had such a jewel in you." Bessie tried to smile. "If only he'd realized it."

"Secretaries are easy to come by," Eleanor reminded her. "Remember the first day I came here, and there were four very efficient ones in front of me for an interview? He won't have any trouble replacing me—he may have already done it for all I know."

"He's hired Betty Maris, is what he's done," Bessie scoffed.

"Miss Betty?" Eleanor blinked. "Old Miss Betty who lives just past Smith's store and raises the African violets and hates men?"

"That's right. Oh, she'll make a dandy secretary, and Curry won't cow her,"

Bessie admitted. "But she's a far cry from you."

"Mandy will love her," Eleanor teased lightly. Her lower lip trembled with tears that wanted to escape. "I'll miss you, Bessie."

"I'll miss you, sugar. Please keep in touch with me. I'll never tell him a thing, I promise," she added knowingly.

Eleanor nodded and, turning to Jim, went quickly out the door without looking back.

The first week was harder than she'd imagined anything could be. Not the work. Jim was patient, and Elaine and Maude and Jeff kept her mind occupied when she wasn't hard at work. But Curry seemed to follow her, always in her mind, on her mind, his face flashing before her eyes, night and day until she thought she'd never again see any peace.

Then, miraculously, after those first days were lived through, she began to lose the paleness and the sparkle came back into her green eyes. It was like living through combat. Taking it one day at a time. She was going to survive it in spite of Curry Matherson.

"Amanda didn't come back with him," Jim remarked over supper one night.

Eleanor concentrated on her mashed potatoes with a vengeance. "Didn't she?"

"Rumor is that he broke the engagement himself."

"Best thing that could have happened," Maude remarked with a nod. "She'd never have made him happy."

"Traveling won't either, but it looks like he's trying it," Jim said as he sipped his coffee. "He'd no sooner got back to the ranch than he took off again. Hasn't come home yet." He frowned. "Maybe the memories are haunting him."

Eleanor knew about haunting, she'd had her share. She could almost feel sorry for Amanda, but the redhead should have known that she couldn't dictate terms to a man like Curry.

"Well, how do you like it here?" Jim asked Eleanor suddenly.

She laughed, gazing around the table to Elaine, Maude and Jeff. "How should I like being surrounded by nice people? None of you turn the air blue, or yell, or threaten to have me drawn and quartered if I don't finish my work exactly on schedule." She glanced at Elaine with a beaming smile. "And I'm having a ball helping Elaine get everything ready for the wedding. I don't even mind addressing invitations."

"Only two more weeks," Jim sighed, his eyes drinking in his pretty fiancée. "How will I live?"

"One day at a time, like the rest of us," Maude laughed.

"I think it's going to be keen, having a mom like the other guys," Jeff volunteered with a wink at Elaine. "I've told everybody."

"I hope I don't disappoint you," Elaine told him with a smile. She was already taken with Jim's son, and it showed. She'd be good for him.

"As long as you don't try to read me any bedtime stories," Jeff cautioned her, "we'll all get along just fine!"

And they all broke up at the plea.

Several days had gone by when Bessie called one night and asked to speak to Eleanor. She'd kept the lines of communication open, but this was the first time Bessie had called at night, and Eleanor had an ominous feeling about it when she picked up the phone.

"Something's wrong, isn't it?" she asked without preamble.

"To my mind, everything is," Bessie admitted with a weary note in her voice. "He's back."

"Jim said he'd been away," came the soft reply, and there was no need to pretend she didn't know who Bessie was talking about.

"Well, he looks like the back end of beyond," the housekeeper said gruffly. "And his temper's so raw I can't even talk to him. Eleanor, I've seen him in all kinds of conditions. Drunk, mad, irritated...but I've never seen him the way he is now. He's pushing himself so hard, I expect any day for one of the boys to bring him in unconscious with a heart attack. I don't know what to do. He won't talk to me, or to anybody else. I'm so worried I can hardly stand it."

Eleanor knew what was coming, and she dreaded the words, but she had to ask, "What do you want me to do?"

"Come over here, and talk to him," she replied, just as Eleanor expected. "He always would talk to you when he wouldn't say a word to anybody else. You can find out what's wrong with him, if anyone can." There was a pause. "Eleanor, we both love that man, despite all his faults. I can almost hate him sometimes, but I can't stand by and let him kill himself. Can you?"

Eleanor stared down at the push buttons on the phone. "No," she admitted weakly. "I can't. When do you think would be a good time?"

"Come to supper. I'll tell him I invited you to come see me. Will you?"

"For you. I'll get one of the boys to drive me over. Bye."

"Thanks, Eleanor. I knew I could count on you."

She hung up the phone with mixed emotions. Could she bear seeing Curry again with all this water under that bridge? Could she bear to hear him pour out the grief that his broken engagement must have caused him? She went upstairs to dress reluctantly. In many ways, this was going to be the hardest thing she'd ever had to do.

It was almost dark when Decker, one of Jim's ranch hands, let her out at the doorstep. The house looked just as she remembered it, big and warm and welcoming with light pouring out the windows onto the ground. If only things had been different, she'd never have had to leave it, she thought wistfully.

She paused on the bottom step to watch Decker drive away, putting off the confrontation until the last possible minute. Then she went up the steps, remembering belatedly that she had to knock on the door now. She couldn't simply walk in as she'd been used to doing before. Everything was different now.

Eleven

She waited breathlessly for someone to answer the door, nervously smoothing the white sleeveless dress down over her hips as she dreaded the sound of booted feet.

But it was Bessie who answered the door, drawing her inside to hug her heartily before she took her into the dining room.

"Curry, I invited company for supper," Bessie called as they went into the dining room, and Eleanor's heart stopped dead as she turned the corner and saw him unexpectedly sitting at the head of the table. She felt as if she'd been shot suddenly, looking straight into those narrow silver eyes without warning.

He looked older, tired, positively haggard, and he'd lost weight. His gaze slid up and down her like an artist's brush, copying every soft line of her body, her face, until his eyes came back up to capture hers and search them.

"If...if you'd rather, I can eat in the kitchen...with Bessie," Eleanor stammered nervously.

He shook his head. "Sit by me," he said quietly, drawing a chair out for her.

Bessie disappeared, leaving her stranded. She laid her purse down in a chair by the door and sat down next to Curry. Her eyes carefully avoided his.

"How are things going?" she asked casually.

"Fine," he replied carelessly. He lifted

his coffee cup to his lips and took a sip of the hot, black liquid. He set it down again. "That's a damned lie," he added quietly. "Nothing's right around here anymore. Is that why Bessie sent for you? Does she really think I need a shoulder to cry on?" he asked in a soft, dangerous tone.

She kept her eyes on the white table-cloth. "She was worried about you; don't be mad at her, Curry."

"Were you worried?"

She kept her face down wordlessly.

He drew in a harsh breath and lit a cig-arette. "No," he said for her. "Of course not, why the hell should you be after the way I treated you? Are you happy, Jade-bud?" he added in a softer tone.

"No," she said involuntarily, letting the word slip out when she'd rather have bitten her tongue off.

"That makes two of us." He reached out suddenly and caught her cool, nerve-less fingers in his. "Honey, if you're not happy now, how can you be happy married to him? Don't jump into anything!''

''Married? Me?'' she exclaimed, meeting his eyes with a puzzled look in her own. ''I'm not getting married.''

''But, Black said....''

''He's marrying Elaine,'' she replied. ''Elaine, whose father owns the Limelight Club,'' she explained. ''They're crazy about each other.''

''Oh. I see,'' he murmured heavily. He took another long draw from his cigarette and meticulously thumped the small ash into the ashtray by his plate. ''Rough, isn't it, Eleanor, wanting something you can't have?'' he asked.

She gaped at him. He thought...he thought she was in love with Jim!

He glanced at her, mistaking the astonishment in her eyes. ''I always could read you like a book,'' he said quietly. ''I've known all along how you felt about him. I'm sorry it didn't work out for you.''

She averted her eyes. ''I'm sorry

things didn't work out for you," she seconded. "I...I heard Amanda didn't come back."

"Hell, I didn't want her back," he said gruffly. "I caught her in her apartment with her photographer. A photographic session, they called it." He grinned like the old Curry. "First time I've ever known it to be done when the photographer and the model had their clothes off."

"Oh," she whispered, reddening.

He glanced at her with a raised eyebrow. "It didn't embarrass me a bit. I took back the ring, wished them luck, and came home."

"Why didn't she tell you the truth?"

"Knowing what I'm worth on the market, you can ask that?" he laughed. "My money has powerful attraction for most women, little one, didn't you know?"

"Only your money?" she asked with a little of her old audacity.

He looked straight into her eyes, and

there was something dark and strange and unreadable in his.

"We made sweet fires that afternoon, didn't we?" he asked her quietly, "and the night before it, too. My women have always been secondhand. It was a first for me as well, touching something innocent, cherishing it.... I'll never forget how soft your skin was, how eager you were to learn what I ached to teach you that night."

She licked her lips to take away the dryness, folding her hands before her on the table to stop their trembling.

"It still embarrasses you to talk about it, doesn't it?" he asked gently.

She nodded, unable to find words enough to answer him. How could she tell him it was the closest she'd ever been to paradise?

"There's something I've got to know," he said with sudden urgency, one of his lean hands reaching over to clasp both of hers.

"That night…was it me you were kissing, or were you pretending I was Jim Black?"

She framed a reply, but Bessie came in suddenly with the first of the supper, and conversation died away under the smell of fresh greens and perfectly cooked beef.

After supper, Bessie tactfully retired to the kitchen, leaving Curry and Eleanor to sit on the front porch where it was cool and quiet.

She sat down in the porch swing, and he took the place beside her, rocking the swing into a lazy creaking motion.

"I've missed you." He said it quietly, and it sounded genuine. "Miss Maris doesn't live in. I can't drag her out of bed at two in the morning to take a letter." He chuckled.

"I was more accommodating," she agreed.

He put a careless arm around her shoulders and drew her against him. "Jim doesn't work you as hard as I did, does he?''

''No.'' She let her head rest on his broad chest, relaxing as she heard the slow, heavy beat of his heart under the cotton shirt, felt the warmth of him enveloping her. He smelled of starch and oriental cologne and tobacco, familiar smells that soothed her. This was magic, what was happening now. Magic, to lie against him and feel his breath on her forehead, and know the sweet security of all that lean strength so close to her.

''Bessie says you're overdoing it,'' she murmured against his shirt.

''She's probably right.'' His arm tightened. ''I hurt, Norie,'' he whispered deeply.

She nuzzled closer, one small hand snaking around his neck to hold him comfortingly. ''I'm sorry,'' she whispered. ''Curry, I'm so sorry it didn't work out for you.''

''Eleanor...'' He hesitated, and she felt

his other hand come up to tilt her face up to his. "I need you...just for a few minutes..."

She read the hunger in his voice, the ache for what he'd lost, the grief...

"Take what you need, Curry," she said quietly, her body yielding to his in an unspoken invitation.

"I won't hurt you..." he whispered unsteadily as he bent to her upturned mouth, feeling it open deliciously as his lips touched it so that the restraint went out of him almost immediately. He lifted her across his knees and kissed her like a drowning man who never expected to feel a woman's softness again. There was desperation in the rough mouth invading hers, urgency. His arms contracted and hurt her, bringing a soft moan from her lips.

"I'm sorry," he bit off against her mouth, relaxing his hold just a little. "Oh, God, I want you so, Norie! I want you so!"

"I can't," she whispered brokenly.

"I'm not asking you to," he said in a husky voice. "I'd never ask that of you."

"But, you said..."

He brought her closer, tucking her face into his throat as he rocked the swing back into motion, cradling her soft body against him in a silence thick with hunger.

"Men are such damned fools," he whispered gruffly. "We never seem to know what we want until it's too late."

"You...you could take her back, you know," she murmured miserably.

"Hell could freeze over, too," he replied. He moved her body against his sensuously. "Soft," he whispered, "soft, like down where you touch me."

She felt the tremors trickling down the length of her body, new and narcotic. "Don't," she protested weakly.

"Another first, little innocent?" he asked at her ear. His mouth slid down to her throat, whispering warmly against it.

His hand slid up her rib cage slowly, feeling her tense and surge up against him as his fingers spread out delicately against her softness. She moaned and tried to draw away.

"You let me do it once," he reminded her softly, "and not through two layers of cloth."

"Curry, don't," she pleaded unsteadily.

"Did you ever let him touch you that way?"

"I've never let anybody…!" she protested, falling right into the trap.

She felt the smile she couldn't see as he gathered her close again and sat just holding her in the darkness.

"I've got to go," she murmured.

His arms tightened possessively. "In a little while. Not yet. Not yet, Jadebud."

She swallowed down the emotions he was arousing. "More games, Curry?" she asked bitterly. "Isn't that where you suggest, casually, that I might like to pack up my broken heart and come back to work for you?''

He stiffened like steel against her.

She pushed away from him and got to her feet. ''That's just what I thought,'' she said, reading his reaction. ''Sorry, I'm not the naïve little girl I used to be, thanks to you.''

''No, by God, you're not,'' he replied, rising to tower over her angrily. ''You've turned into a hard, cynical little hellcat who can't see the forest for the trees. Go back to him and eat your heart out. God knows there's only one way I want you, and it wouldn't be worth the effort at that!''

He turned on his heel and went into his den, slamming the door behind him.

The days seemed to go by in a haze after that. Eleanor felt as if she'd been torn in two, and the half that was left just barely functioned at all. She didn't think she could ever forget the whip in Curry's deep voice as he'd told her bluntly that there was only one way he wanted her, but it wouldn't be worth the effort. Not that she hadn't known that all along. It was so obvious.

But what had he meant, she couldn't see the forest for the trees? That had puzzled her. That, and the fact that he really thought she was in love with Jim. If only it had been true. Loving Curry was a one-way ticket to heartache. She couldn't stop. It had become a way of life over the years, and life without him was as flat as a soft drink left out in the sun.

Every afternoon, she had Decker saddle a horse for her, and she rode. Sometimes it was for a few minutes, others, for an hour or two. And wherever she went on the property that joined Curry's, her eyes searched for him. She'd have given blood for just a glimpse of that tall, commanding figure in the saddle. But it never seemed to happen that way. At least, not at first.

Then, finally, two weeks after the

stormy scene with him, she was riding along the banks of the river when he came upon her on his black stallion, an unexpected confrontation that made her heart race as she drew the chestnut to a halt under a spreading oak.

His eyes were cold as they drifted over her slender figure in jeans and a cool blue cotton blouse.

"Lost?" Curry asked gruffly, a smoking cigarette held loosely between the fingers on his pommel.

She shook her head. "Just riding," she murmured.

"On my land," he told her narrowly.

"I...I thought the river was the boundary," she said in a subdued tone, her eyes drawn involuntarily to the hard masculine lines of his face under the brim of his hat.

"It is, most of the way. But not here." He leaned forward, studying her. "You've lost weight," he remarked quietly. "A lot of it. Doesn't Black feed you?"

"I eat," she replied. She studied his haggard face. "You don't look so terrific yourself."

"I'm pining away for my lost love, didn't you know?" He laughed bitterly. "When's the wedding?"

"Next week. You're invited."

"No thanks," he replied flatly. "I can't stomach the damned ceremonies. What a hell of a way to get a woman into bed."

"He loves her, Curry," she said, meeting his gaze levelly.

"You'd better believe he wants her as well," he returned. "Loving and wanting go together, little girl, for all that you'd like to believe they're completely unrelated."

"I thought you were the one making comparisons between love and the tooth fairy," Eleanor reminded him.

"In the beginning, I did." His pale eyes stared blankly at the river. "I was wrong."

Her heart ached for him. He was hurting in a way she never thought to see him hurt. She hadn't realized how much he'd loved Amanda.

"Oh, Curry, go to her," she said gently, compassion in the look she gave him. "Don't let pride do this to you. Maybe she's just as lonely as you are, did you think about that?"

He stared at her unseeingly. "Pride doesn't have anything to do with it, Jadebud," he said softly. "She doesn't love me."

He said it so simply. *She doesn't love me.* And the pain was in every syllable, in his eyes, his voice, the hardness of his face.

She dropped her own eyes. "I'm sorry."

He drew a deep breath. "So am I. Don't you want to try and console me, little girl?" he asked. "We could console each other. A night in my bed might make your path a little easier, too. I'd make damned sure you didn't have any regrets.''

She gazed at him quietly. ''Do you think that little of me, after all this time?'' she asked him. ''Is that all I am now, a body to satisfy a passing urge?''

His eyes traced her body carelessly. ''What would you like, a declaration of passionate love and a promise of marriage?''

Her eyes flashed. ''Not from you, thanks!''

''Don't worry, I'm not that blind yet!'' he flashed back at her, his eyes cruel.

She flinched. ''Excuse me,'' she said in a choked tone. ''I forgot. You've told me so many times how undesirable I am, I shouldn't have had any trouble remembering.'' She whirled the chestnut and started back the way she came, whipping the animal into a gallop as she reached the pasture.

Her eyes were misty with tears, and she was leaning over the horse's neck, wild to get as far away from Curry as quickly as she could, and she didn't see the gopher hole. Neither did the furiously moving animal, until it caught him and threw him, with Eleanor landing underneath.

The last sensation she had was of crushing pain, and then merciful blackness and oblivion.

The first thing she was aware of was the pressure on her chest. Not hard, not crushing, but pressing against her. There was a voice, too, with anguish in it, murmuring words she couldn't understand, whispering things. Hands touched her, caressed her, and always and forever came that deep, husky voice.

Through the mists of pain, her hands reached up, and buried themselves in thick, cool hair. It was a head pressed against her breasts, hands gripping her back while a voice pleaded with her not to leave him. She couldn't understand who would do that, unless it was her friend Jim....

She licked her parched lips and tried to make a sound. "Jim?" she whispered hoarsely. "Jim?"

The head stilled against her, the hands stiffened and bit into her, hurting her soft flesh. Then the warm contact was suddenly gone, and she wondered vaguely if she'd dreamed it all as she dropped back off again.

A light burned against her eyes. Little by little she came back to consciousness to see a man in a white coat bending over her with a tiny light in a steel cylinder. When her eyes opened, he stood erect and smiled down at her reassuringly.

"How do you feel?" he asked.

She searched herself. "My head hurts," she murmured. She moved in the crisp confines of the white-sheeted bed. "I'm sore...all over."

"I'm not surprised. A horse fell on you." The man, who was obviously a doctor, went out the door and a few seconds later Curry came in. He bent over her, meeting her curious gaze with stormy, dark eyes.

"Are you all right, honey?" he asked softly. "The doctor says I can take you home now as long as someone stays with you for the rest of the night."

She nodded. "Please, I'd like to go home...but, Curry, where is home?" she murmured disorientedly.

"Wherever I am, Eleanor." He brushed the wild, tumbled hair away from her face. "For now, at least. Come on, baby, let's see if you can sit up."

Bessie was waiting on the porch when Curry carried Eleanor up the steps and into the house.

"Hello, sweet," she said, patting the young girl's shoulder. "What can I bring up?"

"Some water and ice," Curry told her. "You'll have to get her into a gown for me."

"I'll get right to it."

Curry climbed the stairs, holding her

close against his taut body, and she leaned back against his broad chest and watched him every step of the way, her eyes quiet and loving.

He looked down into them once and quickly looked away.

"Jim? Will you call him?" she asked.

His jaw clenched. "I already have. I told him I'd take care of you, and he asked me to keep him posted. He's not coming over, if that's what you hoped," he added gruffly.

"I wouldn't expect him to," Eleanor said gently. "Curry, I'm sorry I was so stupid...."

"I drove you to it," he said wearily. "I've done nothing but hurt you for weeks."

She traced a pattern on his shirt with a sharp nail. "It doesn't matter."

"Norie, don't touch me like that," he said in a haunted tone, and she noticed that his breath was suddenly ragged. She looked up in time to see the flash of desire that darkened his eyes as they glanced into hers.

Her lips parted with the strange hungers she was feeling, the dazed condition of her mind making her careless, reckless, as the nearness of him worked on her.

"Like what, Curry?" she whispered, letting her hand slide inside his shirt against the blazing rough warmth of his chest, tangling her fingers in the mat of hair.

A shudder went through him and he crushed her in his arms, bruising her against his body as he went through the doorway to her bedroom and all but threw her onto the bed. He stood over her, breathing harshly, looking down at her with eyes that made her hungry.

"What are you trying to do?" he asked harshly.

She turned her face away from the accusation in his and buried it in the cool pillow. Her head hurt, her heart felt as if it had been blown into splinters.

"I don't know," she whispered shakenly. "I...I wanted to touch you...."

"You took a pretty hard blow on the head," he said tightly. "You've had a mild concussion, baby, it makes you do things you wouldn't normally do."

"That's so," she managed shakily. "I'd never beg you to make love to me if I was myself."

There was a long, static pause. "Is that what you wanted?"

She nodded, her fingers gripping the pillow like a lifeline.

"So that you could pretend I was Jim Black?" he asked bitterly.

"I know who you are, Curry," she told the pillow. She swallowed. "Don't mind me, I'm crazy, isn't that what the doctor told you? Out of my mind with a concussion, and loony. You'd better go before I get up and try to tear your clothes off."

He chuckled softly. "Baby, I'd let you," he said gently. "Any time, any place. But I think it might be better if you healed a little more first, because you're too weak right now for what would happen next.''

She barely heard him. Her dizzy mind was whirling right away from her, and the last thing she heard was the sound of her name being whispered very close to her ear.

She woke up the next morning feeling like a new woman, with no sign of headache, no other symptoms of the concussion she'd suffered.

Her eyes swept the room and found an ashtray beside her bed with a number of cigarette butts in it. She frowned. Only Curry could have done it, but why would he have been sitting by her bed?

The door opened while she sat there puzzling, and she turned her head and looked straight into Curry's amused eyes. He had a mug of coffee in his hand, which he set beside the bed, his eyes tracing the soft lines of her body which were visible through the thin nylon gown.

She followed the direction of his eyes and suddenly jerked the sheet up to her throat with red cheeks.

"Isn't it a little late for that?" he murmured. "I sat here and watched you for the better part of the night. You're very restless in your sleep, little one."

The gown was a little large, and the straps had a disconcerting habit of slipping off even when she was awake. Asleep...she met his teasing gaze and realized that he'd seen a lot more than the gown. The blush travelled down to her neck.

He chuckled softly. "You're lovely to look at, Jadebud," he said. "All pink and soft..."

"Curry..." she began irritably.

He laid a long, brown finger across her lips. "Don't start any fights with me this morning. Last night's too fresh in my memory."

"Last night?" she asked curiously.

One dark eyebrow went up. "Don't you remember what happened?"

She thought for a minute and shook her head. "It's all hazy. What did I do?"

"You tried to undress me," he said matter-of-factly. "Then you begged me to make love to you."

She gasped in horror. "I didn't!"

"Oh, but you did." His eyes smiled at her. "I've never been more tempted to let a woman have her way with me," he added.

"I wouldn't have!" she breathed.

He caught a strand of her hair and tugged on it gently as he sat down on the bed beside her. "You really don't remember?" he probed.

"Honestly, I don't." She saw the humor die out of his eyes, to be replaced by something dark and quiet and intriguing. "Curry, did I really do that?" she asked.

"You wanted it, all right," he said solemnly. "God, so did I, but I'm not such a monster that I'd take advantage of a woman with a concussion.''

"But then you didn't really want me, did you?" she asked unsteadily, her eyes on the sheet. "You've told me so often enough."

He caught her chin and tilted her face up to his. His eyes were dark and quiet. "Haven't you ever heard of camouflage?"

She shrugged. "I suppose."

"I've wanted you for a long time. You can't know how it's been with me these past few weeks." His finger touched her mouth, traced it. "Do you remember that first night you came down the stairs with your hair down and your glasses off— when we'd had the blowup? I stood there and looked at you, and I felt a kind of hunger I never knew I was capable of feeling. But that was just the beginning. It got worse."

Her eyes dropped to his chest. "You felt that way about Amanda," she reminded him.

"No, Norie," he corrected her. "Not after that. Not at all. The night I came home from Houston, when she'd tried her seduction act—I never told you the real reason I walked away from her. It was because I wanted you, and no other woman," he said, meeting her gaze levelly.

Her face mirrored the astonishment she was feeling.

"Curry, I don't understand," she breathed.

"Don't you? And all the time I thought you were eating your heart out for Jim Black. I wanted to break his neck. He could get close to you, and I couldn't. At least, not until the night the bull gored me," he said with a smile. "The first time I kissed you on the porch, I thought he'd been giving you lessons, and when I found out that you were untouched…I had nightmares about what might happen to you with him. The night after I got hurt, I wanted so much to teach you all the things a woman needs to know with a man...I damned near let it go too far. After that, it was a losing battle to keep my hands to myself. When I lapsed, and I did, I took it out on you because I couldn't let you see how much power you had over me.''

"Me?" she asked incredulously.

"Last night," he said quietly, "you did this..." He unbuttoned the top buttons of his shirt, and taking her hand, slid it inside the opening against the moist, bronzed flesh of his body. "It was the first time you ever touched me of your own free will, and you could see the effect it had on me. You wanted me, Eleanor."

She looked deep into his silver eyes, and it all came back. She remembered how she'd felt, what she'd done....

Her fingers moved on his broad chest, touching, loving, exploring.

"I don't want to fight you anymore," she said in a soft, yielding tone.

"What do you want, honey?" he asked gently.

"To love you," she said simply, "for as long as you'll let me."

His eyes searched her flushed face. "Love, in the physical sense or in a deeper sense, Eleanor?"

"Both," she admitted, letting go of her pride as a child might let go of a helium-filled balloon and watch it sail away.

"And if I took you up on that?" he murmured. "If I asked you to come into my bedroom with me, right now, and lock the door?"

She bit her lower lip hard. "I...I'd go," she said, swallowing nervously.

His eyes closed for an instant, as if in relief. "Are you telling me that you love me, Eleanor?"

Tears misted in her eyes. "Didn't you know, Curry?" she asked brokenly. "For three long years!"

He gathered her into his hard arms and crushed her against him, his face buried in the thick, soft hair at her throat. His arms trembled as they contracted around her softness.

"When I got to you yesterday, after the fall," he said huskily, "I held you, listening for a heartbeat that I prayed to hear; begging you not to die. And you reached up to hold my head closer and you said, 'Jim?'" He drew a shaky breath. "And I wanted to ride over a cliff."

"I...I remember," she murmured. "I remember thinking that Jim was the only man who'd care whether I lived or died. I really didn't think it would matter to you."

"If you'd died, I wouldn't have survived you by five minutes," he said matter-of-factly, drawing back to look down into her soft, quiet eyes. "Eleanor, I'm in love with you," he said softly.

The sweetness of those words changed her, brightened her, made her suddenly beautiful. "Oh, Curry..." she whispered.

"We'll talk later," he breathed, bending to her mouth. "Right now, I'm so hungry I can hardly bear it. Come here, honey...."

He brought her up in his arms and kissed her, long and slow and thoroughly, coaxing her slender young hands to unbutton his shirt, to touch him as he caressed her. Fires burned slowly between them until the room seemed to go around in a burst of flame.

"Oh, God, we've got to stop this," he whispered shakenly, putting her from him. He stood up, looking down at his handiwork with eyes full of love as she fastened buttons and blushed under the possessive gaze. "Why don't you marry me?"

"Isn't it a high price to pay?" she teased.

"I want more than your body, little innocent," he told her, and his eyes darkened lovingly. "I want those sons we talked about once. And picnics by the river. Long nights when we can sit together and talk about the good old days. I want everything with you. A lifetime of memories to store day by day.''

''Can we have a church wedding, with all the trimmings?'' she asked.

''And a white gown...if we hurry,'' he added wickedly.

She blushed. ''I'll get Bessie to start on it tomorrow.''

He leaned down and brushed her mouth with his. ''Today,'' he corrected. ''If I remember my 'Cinderella's' correctly, the prince didn't waste any time getting her to the altar when the glass slipper fit.''

He kissed her once, hard, and pulled her up. ''Let's go break the news to your fairy godmother,'' he said with a loving smile. ''Think she'll approve?''

Eleanor tossed her hair and laughed as she hadn't in weeks. ''She'll have to. She loves you almost as much as I do.''

He threw an arm around her shoulder

and led her to the door. "When we break the news we'll go down to the river," he murmured wickedly, "and I'll let you finish what you started last night."

"Only this time," she said grinning, "I won't have a concussion."

He drew her closer beside him. "That's what I'm counting on," he teased gently.

She felt the soft pressure of his mouth at her temple as they started down the stairs.

"Going somewhere?" Bessie asked them as they started down.

"On a picnic," Eleanor said dreamily. "We're getting married!"

"Good for you!" Bessie said with a beaming smile. "Now that you've made the announcement, don't you think there's something you'd better do?"

They stared at her, then at each other.

"Well, Norie, you can't go picnicking like that!" The housekeeper frowned. "What would the neighbors say?"

Eleanor looked down at the pale green gown and sighed. "That," she sighed, "is one black mark in my fairy godmother's book."

And she ran back up the stairs to change, her heart moving to a waltz. The fantasy had become real.

* * * * *

Coming in February 2004
to Silhouette Books

Abandoned at birth, blind genius Connor Quinn
had lived a hard, isolated life until beautiful
Alyssa Fielding stormed into his life and forced
him to open his heart to love, and the newfound
family that desperately needed his help....

Five extraordinary siblings.

One dangerous past.

Unlimited potential.

**A brand-new adventure featuring California's
most talked-about family, The Coltons!**

SWEET CHILD
OF MINE

by bestselling author
Jean Brashear

When Mayor Michael Longstreet and social worker
Suzanne Jorgensen both find themselves in need of a spouse, they
agree to a short-term marriage of convenience. But neither plans
on their "arrangement" heating up into an all-out, passionate affair!

Coming in February 2004.

THE COLTONS
FAMILY. PRIVILEGE. POWER.

If you enjoyed what you just read,
then we've got an offer you can't resist!

Take 2 bestselling love stories FREE!

Plus get a FREE surprise gift!

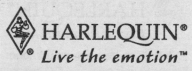

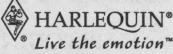